The Games You Cannot Win

A Collection of Short Stories

M.K. Williams

Printed in the United States of America
First Printing, 2016

Publisher: MK Williams Publishing, LLC
Library of Congress Control Number: 2016915862
ISBN
978-0-9967414-7-7

Mary K. Williams

1mkwilliamsauthor@gmail.com
www.1mkwilliams.com

OTHER WORKS BY M.K. WILLIAMS

FICTION
The Project Collusion Series:
Nailbiters
Architects

The Feminina Series:
The Infinite-Infinite
The Alpha-Nina

Other Fiction
Escaping Avila Chase
Enemies of Peace
Interview with a #Vanlifer

NON-FICTION
Self-Publishing for the First-Time Author
Book Marketing for the First-Time Author
How To Write Your First Novel: A Guide For Aspiring
Fiction Authors
Going Wide: Self-Publishing Your Books Outside The
Amazon Ecosystem
Author Your Ambition: The Complete Self-Publishing
Workbook for First-Time Authors

TABLE OF CONTENTS

The Joker - 5
Dolly - 47
Escaping Avila Chase - 123

AUTHOR'S NOTE

When I set out to assemble this collection of stories, I wasn't entirely sure which pieces to include and how to tie them all together. Should I just put together all of the short stories I've ever written into one monster volume, or should I just include the most recent items?

As I finally settled on the list of pieces to be included, the common thread become evident. The stories in this collection were a combination of passion pieces and stories that were just fun to tell. Some were so fluid and easy to write that I struggled to get the words down on paper fast enough, and others went through multiple versions and revisions over the course of 4 years. While the characters each have their own story to tell, they are all struggling with a situation beyond their control. They are thrust into the middle of a game that they cannot see their way out of.

Whether it is career focused, political, personal, or mental: each character struggles with the fact that they are in situation that they can't control and they can't seem to get the upper-hand in. Whether you face a situation where you want to "get ahead" at work, or if you find yourself constantly getting frustrated by politics and pundits, or if you can't stand it when someone you don't have any feelings for tries to meddle in your relationships, try to not let them win. For one moment; close your eyes, take a deep breath, and decide that you don't care. That's right, stop caring about it. Eventually everyone retires, so why put forth the energy on trying to "win" at your career. Inevitably, election outcomes are in the hands of the electoral college and all of our huffing and puffing after the fact won't change the results. Moreover, when someone is trying to get a reaction out of you, the only way to beat them is to not react. So, try not caring. The easiest way to win an unwinnable game, is to not play at all.

When I tried this in my own life I found that I suddenly had more energy to devote to my dreams. I had the courage to write the stories that just needed to be told without caring whether a critic liked the final outcome. I stopped worrying that a story that I just wanted to tell might be read as a personal attack on someone else. I know it isn't, so I stopped caring if someone else extracted their own interpretation. They were going to do that anyway.

The marvelous thing about exiting from the games that seem to run our society, is that it frees up so much energy. Time and worry are two things that will never be refunded, even once you feel like you've won. If you want to find a way to channel your efforts into something positive and worthwhile, try a charity.

The final story in this series: *Escaping Avila Chase*, was

by far the most fun to write and also the most ambiguous. At times I had a sinister ending all planned out, only to replace it with something sweet and sappy, before going back to darker content. A conversation with a good friend of mind last winter gave this story the ending it needed. My friend inspired the unnamed character who is speaking at the book launch in the story. The character was a woman who worked for a non-profit aimed at helping children lost to human-trafficking. My friend traveled to India to help out with the current efforts to stop the cycle. She learned about the systematic issues in place that need to be resolved and the different elements of life inside the brothels that are so particularly brutal.

She told me her story, I thought to myself, it's like a game you can't win. There is too much to be done, and so many already impacted by it. My pessimism only lasted for a moment as her story continued to give me hope and inspire me to try to focus my efforts on a more worthwhile cause.

Imagine if we all laid down our smaller troubles: will I get a promotion, will so-and-so start to respect me, will they just move on already, and began to focus on the global issues that actually threaten our humanity. What if we all worked together to end the systemic issues of human trafficking and stopped worrying about our little daily battles. How much better would our world be? How much better would we feel?

If you want to start to take action, visit Effect.org. Whether you want to travel to Nepal or India to help onsite, or if you just want to share their mission with your friends on social media, every little bit can help. Every action towards that mission helps us to all win the only battle that matters: human rights.

The Games You Cannot Win

To my mother,
author of The Next Great American Story

THE JOKER

The slick tiled floor gave way to a thin beige Berber carpet immediately upon exiting the elevator. A large and chunky, bright yellow cart rolled out slowly from the elevator car onto the solid floor. Maneuvered with great effort by a man that was only 39, but looked as though he was in his late 50s, the cleaning cart wheels squealed and squeaked under the weight of the vessel and the 90-degree angle being attempted by the janitor.

Randolph tipped back in his desk chair, straining his neck to see around the corner. As he leaned he could see that the noise that he and his pals had just heard was Oleg, part of the nightly cleaning crew, coming to make his rounds. Randolph's straight brown hair flopped back and forth as he leaned back then returned the chair legs to the floor. Once centered, the bangs of his bowl-cut hair formed a pattern on his forehead. *Perhaps an inverted diamond, or the appearance of fangs*, thought Tyler, one of the other men at the table.

"Yeah well there is always an angle," Milton finished his comment as Oleg pushed his cart past the bank of desks and computers, along the main thoroughfare of the office. Milton, the wise and seasoned veteran among them, played out his hand. He waved to Oleg who continued on with a small acknowledgement to the group. Milton made a habit of greeting everyone who walked by. He was just a friendly guy, and he didn't want to be seen as a jerk if he excluded someone. Milton didn't want his motives questioned, so he waved to everyone.

Randolph had regained his normal posture and focused on the deck of cards in his hand. He and Milton were up, but Gregory and Tyler could take the lead in the next bid. Randolph didn't want to lose. Not for pride or love of the game, but because he hated buying beer for other people, and that's what was at stake. Milton kept his face calm and had an overall devil-may-care appearance. His salt-and-pepper hair was always a little wonky, as though he slept with his wet hair pressed up against his pillow. Gregory and Tyler however, were all business; their eyes were focused on the space where Randolph would lay his cards. They weren't diverting their attention from the matter-at-hand.

As 'the fellas' played out their last hand, Oleg began to polish the Peabody's and Pulitzers that lined the hallway down to the breakroom, before setting off to vacuum the entire floor.

The hand of Bridge was finished and Gregory and Tyler stood slowly to accept their defeat. With the sound of raucous heckling, they headed to the elevators to brave the cold and purchase a six-pack of beer for

Randolph and Milton.

The two remaining men gathered the cards and Randolph began to shuffle them in his hand.

Riffle, bridge.

Riffle, bridge.

Riffle, bridge.

Milton turned his chair around and faced his computer. He shook his electronic mouse vigorously (he had a real mouse in his apartment, it was not a pet) to interrupt the screensaver. Before him was a mess of words and information that had only 4 more hours to be turned into a printable and newsworthy article.

"You know each time I come back to my desk, I am disappointed to see that these words haven't rearranged themselves while I was away." Milton shook his head and motioned at Randolph.

Randolph shook his head as well, a sympathetic reflex. He hardly noticed that he was mimicking Milton because it wasn't a conscious action. He continued to shuffle the pile of cards as he thought of a verbal response; he couldn't let a silence go uninterrupted.

Riffle, bridge.

Riffle, bridge.

Riffle, bridge.

"Well, maybe one day they will surprise you Milton," Randolph offered a nonsensical alternative.

"They'd better, those lazy bastards!" Milton was known for being dogmatic, it was part of his charm, if it could be considered charming at all. He was at the age where he could make bad jokes and have them pass as 'dad-jokes' or the good humor of an old man trying to be funny. He was making some really horrible puns lately, but everyone just shook their head and laughed at how awful his humor was rather than telling him to stop.

"The words aren't lazy; your story is just shit!" Randolph snickered while Milton picked up some stray paperclips and chucked them at his colleague.

"Yeah, well I can't help it. I can't stand working this beat anymore!"

"Well don't tell that to Gregory or Tyler, they would kill to lead on the election." Randolph pointed out the obvious truth. Writing for the political section of their newspaper was considered the peak of the profession. (And Tyler was particularly ambitious when it came to what he perceived as helping his career.)

They were employed by one of the most well respected newspapers in publication, still turning a profit, and their political coverage were considered to be bar-none in the industry. Milton might be a sly card player, but he was considered one of the best journalists in the country, and had numerous awards to prove it. His modest wardrobe and humble manner were executed perfectly. He never came off as too aloof, nor did he seem to be too proud of himself. Milton was the paragon of reserved professional excellence. Randolph always felt humbled to be able to work with him, though he would never actually say that to Milton's face. *Maybe at his retirement party*, Randolph rationalized.

"Good, let them!" Milton returned to his screen. "Let them report daily on the inane childish behavior of presidential candidates for the two and a half years that they run!" Randolph knew that Milton was set off, he braced for the rant. "The election is every four years, they spend more than half the time between elections campaigning! And the way they talk to each other and about each other, goodness they could all use some time in a charm school!"

Randolph knew the next statement that would set Milton spinning, he was a predictable man. Gregory and Tyler loved to prod at Milton until he spewed out his usual rhetoric. In their absence, Randolph delivered the line that would trigger Milton's ire. "Well, surely one of them is worthy of the office of the President." Randolph couldn't hide the smile on his face as he said it, anticipating Milton's next response. Riffle, bridge. He shuffled the cards feigning a blameless shrug, but he knew full-well what his words would inspire.

"Oh, don't even get me started-" Milton stopped himself before such an event could occur and threw a 'I know what you're trying to do' smirk at Randolph before spinning his chair around fully to face his computer screen again. Milton clacked at a few of the keys and then spent a moment or two focused on the pencil that he set on the bridge of his nose. *Will it fall, will it balance?* The age-old procrastination technique was still in play.

Randolph finished his shuffling and stood, leaving the cards on the table before maneuvering his desk chair back to the empty computer across from Milton's desk. Randolph, the lowly fact-checker of the team, was glad to be included in the group of journalistic giants that he had the opportunity to work. And play card-games like Bridge with. Gregory and Tyler were a few years his senior and were quickly becoming the well-respected up-and-comers who had paid the down payment on their career 'dues.' Randolph was keen to learn from all of the men on his team, but he was most interested in gaining the approval and respect of Milton.

Randolph interrupted his screensaver and saw that his email inbox had received a deluge of new requests for verification on stories that were scheduled to print the next day. He started with the first one and began to work through his usual process. Since starting at the newspaper several months earlier, he had been exhausted, burned from boiling hot coffee, called the wrong name by everyone at least once, and profoundly inspired by his colleagues.

He was inspired to leave the field of journalism. Or at least he was contemplating it seriously. The devil on his shoulder whispered of higher paying opportunities.

Randolph reached for his headphones and resumed the track that had been paused before the bridge game had started. The loud and shrill screams picked-up, as did the snare. Milton could hear the faint pulsing of the music coming out of the headphones. He marveled at how the young man had any hearing left given the decibels being pounded against his ear drums.

Randolph set off to get some work done, but his thoughts remained on the most pressing dilemma on his mind: what to do with his empty dream of a career. The only reason he was sticking it out was that he had managed to sit next to one of the writers that he had idolized during his college career. *How could he walk away, when he sat just a few feet from the man he had wanted to become?* Randolph's angst was a disillusionment born from missing out on a bygone era. Randolph longed to relive the glory days of reporting with Milton. Instead, he was left with the pyrite luster at the fall of the empire: all hedonism and no sound reasoning to hold up the walls of Mother Liberty any longer. His dream appeared to him as if it were the tail end of a brush stroke; dry and constantly reaching out, the fibers begging for color, but coming up short and white on the canvas.

The glimmer of a career as a journalist wore off once he entered the real game. Keywords and impressions were dressed up words for: only write what people want to read, get more eye-balls onto your article, that is all that matters. Sure, there were occasionally a few profound pieces set to be published, but those were only read by those who were in earnest pursuit of the news. Most people just skimmed and forgot what was being published very quickly.

Randolph couldn't blame the entire newspaper industry for that though, the culture was shape-shifting around them and they were trying to keep up. It still made him sad to think that he might write the most insightful article and it would be noticed by only the few who still bothered to even read the news. The real news, not just the tabloids. He was suffering from anticipatory disillusionment. Randolph's pre-defeated, millennial attitude was starting to annoy himself; he focused back on the task at hand.

Just outside of his peripheral view, Milton had given up on trying to balance that pencil and had turned his attention to his article. After some sips of stale coffee, he made an expressive gesture and a wrenching sound.

"Bleh! Cold coffee that tastes like ass!" Milton stood up with his coffee cup in hand. Randolph swiped his headphones from his ears just in time to catch the end of Milton's remark.

"Come on, I'll get a fresh pot started," Milton was headed down the row of desks that comprised the bull-pen. The music continued to travel out of his headphones and fill the small space around Randolph with the shrill sound of distorted voices and loud drums. Randolph wasn't interested in drinking any coffee, he truthfully hoped that he would be on his way home in an hour and wanted to be able to fall asleep and stay asleep. He hadn't been getting much quality sleep since the Presidential debates had begun a few months earlier. Randolph was constantly worried that he was missing something; a new sound bite that was potentially explosive, a political development that would require a statement from each candidate, anything to help him cast his first big story. The twenty-four-hour news-cycle that applied to all media outlets seemed to be somehow amplified, to have a large inertia in the political world. The stakes always seemed higher, the fate of one country or many countries were implied to be in the balance. But lately Randolph had been wondering, are they really?

The more he read, and wrote, and checked, it seemed that the political figures were only a physical representation of an ideal that had long lost its status. They were placeholders on a decimal that was now too small to matter. Were these men and women really moving the needle on any one initiative or were they just a focal point, a distraction while the political grunts and greedy tricksters ran the economy. Basically like a magician trying to divert your attention from the trick? Randolph was toying with his apathy, but he knew that would only land him into the same cycle that most Americans were stuck in: unenthused and indebted.

To avoid this feeling, he remained steadfast in his work, and that meant following the Rock-God that was his boss and mentor, Milton, to get coffee at quarter-til 10.

Milton was always a quick walker, and when he was determined to get a caffeine fix, he walked exponentially faster. Randolph fell a little behind as he mulled the frustrations in his mind.

The new filter was being placed into the coffee maker, the ground coffee waiting to be brewed, and Milton's eyes were drying imperceptibly when Randolph entered the empty and freshly cleaned break-room. Milton wordlessly moved to the refrigerator in the corner. There had been two refrigerators, but a lingering smell had begun to emanate from one. As they say, all the king's horses and all the king's men couldn't get the old frumpy fridge to smell clean again. Now there was just one fridge in the corner, humming as the electric power kept the machine working.

Milton reached for one of the tall bottles of brand name creamer. There were several that were commonly shared by the team. At least, that is what Milton assumed as no one had ever marked these flavored bottles, no one had chastised him for using them, and they were always replenished. Milton shrugged his shoulders at the thought and assessed the options before him.

Randolph leaned against the door frame, mentally checking off items on his to-do list. Milton held-up two creamer bottles and called to Randolph, "Hey, which flavor do you think?"

"I'm not having any," Randolph pulled his jowls down into a low but passive snarl with his nose pulled up, commonly referred to as 'stank face.' This, however, was a polite stank face as if to indicate, 'no thanks.'

"Oh, well I'm working on a piece about Nuthead, so I'll go with Hazelnut." Milton picked the bottle with the red topper.

"Sounds fair," Randolph appreciated the humor in Milton's decision process.

"Yeah, I wish Pierrot would do something other than look like a dope. Then I could have the French Vanilla."

"Good point, maybe we can dig up some dirt on him just so you can enjoy a new creamer."

"Eh, but Nuthead was made to make headlines."

All of the candidates had nicknames. Milton enjoyed giving them out. He still referred to the current President as Doobie McGee and various ex-candidates by their not-so-affectionate pet names that he had appointed at one time or another. Milton still hadn't lost his edge: Hapless Wonder, Pierrot, Nuthead, and Hapless Idiot were the most discussed of the current field of candidates.

Hapless Wonder received his nickname because Milton thought that in the end this candidate would win out, and how unfortunate for that person that they would actually become President. However, Hapless Wonder had bowed out of the election only a week earlier, much to the chagrin of the moderate electorate.

Nuthead was thus named because his head looked like that of a Kukui nut; he also seemed to be the most in need of clinical diagnosis.

Pierrot was deemed absolutely unlikely to win or be anywhere near a ballot in November, but Milton was thoroughly amused when he had made the connection that the politician looked like the French sad mime-clown, and enjoyed bringing it up as often as possible.

Then there was Hapless Idiot, which started out as the nickname for the junior Senator from Milton's home state, but soon grew to encompass the rest of the unremarkable field. The rest didn't get too much of a mention. Pantsuits was keeping out of the news, which meant no bad news, but also meant no attention for their campaign. Lazy-Eye was the most apt nickname for the reformed philanderer from the Bible Belt. That was the least polite of the nicknames, so Milton usually referred to this person by their last name in staff editorial meetings. When he was just talking bylines with the guys, he was less considerate.

Milton poured his coffee, mixed in the creamer and sugar, then savored a few sips while leaning against the countertop.

"Ok, he is a total nut job, but if it means I get to enjoy more hazelnut flavored items, I guess he's not so bad." The lower half of Milton's face disappeared behind his coffee mug, leaving his wise eyes and graying eye brows just visible above the porcelain rim.

"If his only redeeming quality is a food superstition, that's not a very good reason to elect." Randolph countered. "But now I am craving some Nutella."

"True," Milton nodded. "Hah, if he wins I'll start calling the first lady Nutella. Great idea!" Milton toasted Randolph who accepted by saluting dimly, letting his hand fall mid-flight.

"Do you think he could really win?" Randolph asked, scared that the seasoned journalist would provide a prophetic answer that would disappoint his last idealistic molecules.

"I don't know. I think he is enough of a distraction that no one, from either party, is getting much attention on their platform."

Randolph silently nodded, agreeing that the campaign had been more like a bid for an Oscar nomination with a lot of star power and coverage, but with an air of triviality. It felt worse this time around, more meaningless than ever before. The reality of the impoverished, hungry, and war-torn seemed to matter less than they did in 2012; which wasn't much in comparison. Randolph earnestly tried to run through a list in his mind of where each candidate stood on education reform and declining literacy rates, gun violence and the indifference towards mental illness, the government's inability to pass a simple budget, a never-ending war with no purpose and no defined objectives, and the ever-enraging socialized health care system. Randolph could think along party lines where the candidates would be ideologically, but hadn't actually heard any of them address a plan for what they would do to remedy the most pressing domestic issues. He began to shake his head slowly, unable to believe that his life-long ambition of covering politics had revealed the whole system as a three-ring circus. Each party was trying to lure people into their tent and fool them with their vaudevillian stage-magic.

Milton continued to sip his coffee and examined his young colleague. Thin, overly-tall, and with the overly rehearsed impression of upper-class upbringing, Randolph was clearly a poor boy in a sophisticated man's world. His real name was Michael Randolph Jones. Sounded W.A.S.P-y enough, but he insisted on being called Randolph because growing up he had been called

"Mikey." This alone wasn't necessary a sign of being a poor-kid, but it didn't have a professional tone either. Milton wanted to tell him that Randolph didn't sound very professional either, it almost sounded too snooty, but he knew that the kid was trying to fit in, so he let it go.

"Who do you think will win it, kid?" Milton asked as he swallowed the last gulp of his coffee.

Randolph let out a deep sigh, like a wounded and moody teenager. "Will I seem like a complete snob if I say that I don't think the American public is smart enough to discern between a ruse and a real leader?"

"No, that wouldn't make you sound like a snob if you said it that way." Milton began to wash out his mug. "But if you said it like this," Milton began to elongate his vowels and added a posh New England accent to his words, "then you would sound like a snob."

Randolph laughed at Milton's humor. "Scary enough, I think Nuthead might win it."

"So, what then?" Milton asked as he dried the mug and set it up in the cupboard.

"Maybe a request to work abroad. Or just up and move to Costa Rica." Randolph smiled at the idea of days lounging in the shade of massive banana leaves.

"Why Costa Rica? And why do you think he will win?"

"Seriously, have you read anything about Costa Rica? It is the most perfect country with the best beaches in the world, 95% literacy rate, and no standing army." Randolph began to sound excited about something for the first time in months. *Perhaps*, he wondered, *he should switch from politics to travel writing*. But, if there was one beat more cut-throat than politics, it was the travel section.

"Sounds amazing! Ok, so the Costa Rica answer makes sense now. I will have to brush-up on my Central American paradises." Milton passed to the doorway and led Randolph back down the hallway towards their desks. "Now, why do you think Nuthead will win?" Milton was trying to get more out of the kid, he could see the growing signs of apathy. Randolph was smart and had a lot of potential. Milton had been able to weather many political crises and scandals without too much of his faith in democracy being waivered. He could see the kid was losing his fast; Randolph wouldn't last long without a basic belief in justice.

"Just something about him. It's almost too scary to think that so many people are rooting for him. He has too much momentum to be stopped." Randolph stated plainly.

Milton shrugged his shoulders while his hands rested in his two front pockets. "Well, we've just got to keep informing the people about what really does matter and hope that they will follow that to make the best decision possible."

Randolph nodded. They both took a seat at their respective desks and were about to resume their late evening routine that would lead them down to the wire, right up until the deadline when Milton would submit his story. Randolph would finish some more work, and they would head out together for their evening cigarette. Randolph had come to enjoy the routine with his mentor, each moment more unrealistic than the next. He may have been waning in his enthusiasm for politics, but the admiration he had for his mentor was off the charts.

"Well, let's hope one candidate can knock him out of contention. I don't care which party at this point, although it would be nice to see the Dems win it." Randolph was resigned to his default hopes and the late-night exhaustion had his spirits beat.

Milton typed in a few keystrokes to unlock his computer, which had gone into the self-protected screen saver phase automatically. "Hah, yeah. But the way Nuthead is leading the crazy brigade and making everyone hate the Reps, the Dems couldn't have paid for a better outcome. Might as well sit back and let the self-destruction of the Grand Ole Party start. Am I right?" Milton was smiling and didn't look over at Randolph as he made his joking comment. If he had been looking at the young man, he would have seen his easy smile quickly change into a flummoxed frown.

"Right," Randolph said in response, almost a beat too late, but Milton was busy finishing his article and didn't notice. Milton also didn't notice Randolph's change in energy level. It was very quickly renewed and almost radiating from him, a pulsing aura of kinetic motion. Randolph was quickly typing, searching, and scribbling quickly with his pencil on a stack of post-its. Milton almost didn't notice when Randolph quickly printed a few documents and then stood to shut off his computer and grab his coat.

"Leaving already?" Milton asked. He tried to sound like he was giving the kid a hard time. He didn't want to seem like a hard-ass that expected him to stay until all hours every night. But Milton didn't want to seem too careless about it either.

"Yeah, it's almost 11 and I have a few things to check on before tomorrow." Randolph was busy gathering a few items from his desk hastily and shoved his laptop into his over-shoulder messenger bag. Milton could see that Randolph was in a hurry. Really, he was more than 'in a hurry', Randolph was in a frenzy, the kind that only a powerful idea can create.

Perhaps that lower-middle-class upbringing had engendered an overall mistrust of those with money and those who had control over mass-sums of it. Maybe it was that inherent bias left Randolph susceptible to the idea now growing in his mind. Susceptible and willing to see it through to the end. Perhaps that chip on his shoulder was his edge, his angle all along. Randolph was running with an idea, now feeling the pressure that at any moment someone else could discover the same thought. Time was his enemy now, Randolph would have to work against the clock.

"Okay then, see you tomorrow." Milton tried to seem buried in his article because he didn't want to sound like he was worried about Randolph, but he was.

"Yeah, bye." Randolph was gone and nearly knocked

into Gregory and Tyler as he rushed out of the building. When the two gents returned to their desk with the required beers they asked Milton what was up with Randolph. Milton shrugged his shoulders and said, "No idea," before returning to his article and pressing send. The remaining journalists enjoyed the beers and played Rummy, because they were one player short for Bridge. They finished their drinks, won their rounds, and headed home; ready to start the whole process again the next day.

The next day did arrive without much commotion. No countries had gone into civil war, no bomb had been dropped on innocent people, and no well-paid ex-mistress had come forward with her story. This is what a slow news-day always started out as, and it almost always preceded an event that would shake up the world. Or it would be just another day. In his younger years, Milton would relish in the added energy and excessive adrenaline of those big stories, those news events. Recently, he had grown tired of them. *How many mass-bombings would he see in his lifetime, how many despots that were undeniably corrupt would remain in power, how many deaths would be added onto the un-ending stock pile of madness in this world?* Milton didn't have the answers, but the growing calm in the office was providing a sense of unease, of unnecessary malaise; he was a little on edge because of the lull.

By 1 pm the news day had remained slow and Milton pulled up some older files that contained unpolished editorials. These articles just needed a little bit of love, as

Milton would commonly say. He had a reservoir of ever-green articles that would just need a little cleaning up to be submitted. He saved them for days such as this.

The only noteworthy item that day was the obvious and unexplained absence of Randolph. His desk was eerily empty, his screen completely blank. Milton wasn't in the habit of covering for people or throwing them under the bus, so when he was asked directly, "Hey, where is Randolph?" he said, "I don't know," and continued his work. No need to speculate as to his whereabouts or editorialize his presumptive excuses. Milton left the creativity to his writing. He did wonder if Randolph had caught onto a story that would put him in danger. Most politicians were egomaniacs and a few of the rougher ones were known to bully the media. Milton didn't want Randolph to experience that side of the journalistic world just yet.

At quarter 'til two Milton's cell phone buzzed discretely beneath a pile of notes. He swiped and read through the text that Randolph had sent. "Working on some facts to check, will be in for tonight's game." Milton almost chuckled at the kid's bravado. Milton knew that he had to set a good example while also telling him to keep at it. "Be sure to text Brandt so he knows you're not a no-show. Have fun finding those facts. See you later." Brandt was the human resources manager who was a stickler for docking sick-days and reporting even the smallest violations to the employee handbook. Milton didn't agree with his methods, but the whole company had to live with them. He pressed send on his text response to Randolph.

Milton's reply was equally vague and conversational. *Had Randolph been out pondering his career? Was he interviewing for a normal nine-to-five that wouldn't allow him to hone his journalistic skills?* Milton's mind only wandered for a moment, then he returned to the story that he would inevitably procrastinate until all hours of the evening.

And so he did. Pencil balanced on the bridge of his nose, Gregory and Tyler smack-talking about their yet-to-be-realized win in Bridge, and the story completed at the stroke of midnight, Milton dallied and delayed as was his routine. But, Randolph never showed. Tyler had texted him to see if he was still coming in; there was no response. Milton was a little uneasy, Randolph wasn't in the habit of being a flake and he had specifically stated that he would be back in the office that evening. *Where was Randolph, and what was he up to?* A lifetime of poorly executed conspiracies had tempered Milton's ever-present suspicious tendencies, but this qualified as a "something is up" moment.

The next morning Milton arrived to the office, groggy and nursing his dry and itchy eyes by applying over-the-counter eye drops while walking off of the elevator. He blinked in the relief and wiped the stray liquid away from his face so that no one would think that he was being emotional or welling-up with tears. He jostled his way past coworkers, all of them barely visible through the blur of the eye drops.

Milton's vision restored just as he rounded the corner and walked into the main work-area. He saw a sad looking lump at Randolph's desk. It appeared that the young fact-checker had in-deed arrived at the office, but so late into the evening that he was really only a good 6 hours early for work.

Milton let his worn leather messenger-bag slouch onto the ground with a weak and muffled thud. The requisite leather bag of a journalist, holding Milton's mole-skinned notebook, he was outfitted as any good reporter should be. For a 'coming-out-swinging' left-wing liberal, Milton sure was surrounded by bound animals. The subtle noise of the bag dropping didn't rouse Randolph.

Milton whipped his rain-jacket off, trying to make it as noisy as possible, but the nylon fibers were so sleek that they only made a ruffle. As Milton turned on his computer and sat in his chair, his subtle attempts to wake Randolph were an absolute loss. So he tried the obvious old-guy method and cleared his throat very loudly as he perched his feet on his desk and leaned back far into his chair.

This was what caused Randolph to slowly move, then very quickly dart his head up to see that it was morning, and that light was pouring into the office. But he shot his head up too quickly and pulled his neck; reflexively his right palm moved to sooth the muscle.

"So, late night?" Milton asked, knowing the answer, but also expecting this to prompt Randolph into a detailed explanation. He had instinctively taken a paternalistic tone, but he tried to make his voice sound as though the comment was ironic. He understood that kids were all about irony now-a-days.

"Yeah, you could say that." Randolph rubbed his neck with one hand and his eyes with another.

Milton waited for additional elaboration. It was not forthcoming.

"Well," Milton broke the silence. "What do you have to show for it?"

Randolph was still visibly distracted or just not fully awake yet. "Uh, would you mind reading something over if I printed it out for you?"

"As long as it has everything to do with why you were completely absent yesterday." Milton made sure that there was no question that he was not pleased with Randolph's flakey behavior.

"Oh it does," the kid's eyebrows were animated with excitement.

"Okay, I'll read it," Milton shrugged his shoulders, put his feet back on the floor, and turned to face his work station.

"Awesome!" Randolph showed his age more and more with those easy adjectives. "I'm going to grab a coffee; you want one?"

"Sure," Milton was reflexively scanning through his emails and had already turned his attention from whatever trouble Randolph was obviously working himself into.

Within fifteen minutes, the kid had returned with two

piping hot mugs of coffee, both flavored with Hazelnut creamer, and a thin stack of papers. Randolph left one mug of coffee on Milton's desk, just in front of the papers that he had spent all night working on.

Milton tried to look mildly uninterested and took a few sips of coffee before reaching for the papers. Randolph nervously watched Milton during this expanse of time, and he didn't care at all how odd it appeared for him to be staring at Milton so obviously. Randolph was a man on a mission and wanted to make sure that what he had uncovered was appreciated.

Milton began to read what was in front of him. "This is an article. Randolph, you wrote an article?"

"Yes, sir. Researched it and wrote it myself." Randolph curtly nodded his head in the affirmative.

"Then why does the byline have both of our names on it?" Milton turned the front page around to show Randolph what he knew was already there.

"Well the most basic reason is credibility. But you also gave me the idea for it." Randolph took a sip of coffee quickly after he said this to hide the embarrassment on his face. Milton gave him a 'you had better have a good reason for all this nonsense' look and then resumed reading.

"I can tell it is your first piece, too much metaphor here at the beginning. How about you just tell me what this is about and then I can help you edit it?" Milton didn't have the time to make good on this offer to read the article, but he did want to know what Randolph had skipped out on work to do. He could read through five pages of obscure references that Randolph had layered around the actual meat of his story after he heard what the kid had to say.

"Okay," Randolph said nervously, he tried not to look hurt by Milton's quick dismissal of his crafted words. Randolph quickly looked around his desk as though he would need a prop, after shuffling through some papers he stopped and took a deep breath. "How many political ads have you seen this year?"

"None, I'm always at work." Milton responded before the question could even really settle in.

"Ok, think about the last time you were at home and watching TV, any ads?" Randolph needed Milton to see this first point.

"We never get those ads, they don't bother with them in New York City, they know how we will vote." Milton was correct on that point. The majority of the advertising dollars went to the much-contested areas and the swing-states. Randolph's recent escapades into fact-finding had confirmed this.

"OK, right?" Randolph followed with this space-filler of a question. Milton had responded exactly how Randolph had planned, so far so good. "So, I called my Grandma living down in Boca. They get hit with millions of ads the second the first person announces their candidacy. You follow?"

"Sure," Milton was not dazzled by what Randolph was saying yet and his voice showed it.

"Ok so this year she says she has seen a few for Hapless Wonder; positive, very Christian, very sweet, and an unimaginable amount for Nuthead."

"Well he is independently wealthy, he can afford a lot of ad time. Shouldn't he be focused on Iowa though?" Milton was busy ticking off dates of primaries and caucuses in his mind as Randolph continued.

"That's what I thought too, so I called up my college roommate who is working the caucus in Des Moines-" Randolph started to pace as he explained his thought-process.

"Geesh kid, do you know someone in all 50 states?" Milton retorted sarcastically.

"And Guam! Listen," Randolph emphasized his plea with his arms and his head leaning toward Milton, "it's somewhat different in Iowa with some ads for most of the GOP ticket, almost none for the DNC, and then so many for Nuthead that my buddy practically doesn't even get to see his regular TV shows anymore."

"Again, he's rich." Milton wasn't trying to make the kid feel bad, but he knew the level of scrutiny needed to publish, and so far this wasn't cutting it.

"Right," Randolph was happy that Milton had responded as expected so far, "so I looked a little further. We work for a media group, which means the holding company that owns us also owns the companies that distribute national and regional TV ads."

"Hmm, I'm with you," Milton started to become more intrigued. Usually where there is a conglomerate there is a good news piece. Most are benign, but the public generally distrusts them, the title itself is pretty cringe-worthy. Conglomerate. Conglomerate. It always made Milton think of the sound that room-temperature grape jelly makes when it is slapped onto a piece of bread. Gooey, squishy, and moist.

"So I did some digging-" Randolph began to elaborate.

"Legal digging?" Milton didn't want to hear about something he would have to testify on later, or at the least be called into the editor's office for.

"Sure." Randolph was taken by this question, but it only shook him for a moment, then he batted it away with his quick answer, ready to get to the point.

"Ugh," Milton slapped his hand over his face. His patience was starting to become expended.

"Listen, I did some digging and Nuthead paid for all of the ads himself in each of the swing states." Randolph seemed to be elated by the fact. Milton was less then enthused.

"OK, that's not news." Milton began to turn back to his computer screen, moments away from going idle and locking.

"No, but the sum total paid for those ad is more than what his entire annual income was last year." Randolph waited for Milton's reaction, there was none. "All the candidates released their income tax records." Randolph handed some of his stack of loose papers from his desk over to Milton.

"So, he has donors." Milton flipped through the figures quickly.

"Yes and he has to disclose that as well. His donors paid for those God-awful wristbands and trucker hats and that double decker campaign bus. The commercials were paid for from his personal checking account." Randolph pointed to invoices that he pulled from their sister company, how he got them Milton did not want to know.

"Well maybe-" Milton began to respond with an off-the-cuff plausible explanation, but Randolph was really going now and cut him off.

"So, I dug a little further into his travel schedule, and that of the DNC chairwoman."

Milton leaned his head, indicating his interest in hearing the next sentence out of Randolph's mouth.

"They don't intersect- at all." Randolph seemed to be very solemn about this fact as well.

"OK, more non-news." Milton threw his hands up in the air, the financial statements still firmly in his right hand.

"Except, Nuthead was dumb enough to check-in on Facebook at the Mall of America with the caption 'This is why America is so great!' on August 18th, three days before he officially announced his candidacy." Randolph showed a print-out of the photo to Milton.

"But he had already begun campaigning by then," Milton finished the sentence for Randolph.

"Yes, but that was calm and somewhat collected Nuthead. He was being diplomatic; he was calm in his interviews. As compared to today when he acts like he is having a nervous breakdown with delusions of grandeur." Randolph continued their joint thought a little further.

"Accurate, go on." Milton liked Randolph's apt description of Nuthead and wondered how he could weave it into a story without being hit with a slander claim.

"Well the DNC chairman did officially travel to Bloomington, Minnesota on August 17th, she stayed for two days and was pictured with her family on the carousel at the mall." Randolph had an official looking photo for that as well.

Milton looked at the two photos, trying to see how a coincidence could be made into a bona fide connection. "OK so two proud Americans visited an American landmark."

"But then why is it off of Nuthead's official travel records?" Randolph finally arrived at the end of his planned conversation and now entered the realm of connecting the final dots.

"Because he wasn't a candidate at that point, at least not officially." Milton was about ready to hand everything back to the kid and tell him to get back to work.

"No, because they wanted to hide a meeting. They met when they were both in town." Randolph was emphatic on this point.

"So why did they meet?" Milton asked to humor Randolph, but his tone was short and blunt.

"OK, so you want to know why they met?" Randolph

was not good with 'winging-it' and it showed.

"Yes, I just asked you that. I don't like to ask questions twice, especially when I am on a deadline here kid!" Milton was practically yelling, he tried to modulate his tone.

"The DNC has to provide record of where they spend their money. According to the records I was able to acquire-"

"Legal?" Milton asked again, frustrated that his time and good humor had been wasted.

"They have been spending like crazy, but have you seen any ads for a Dem candidate? Any posters, or stickers, or buttons?" Randolph could tell that he only had a few seconds left before Milton just walked away.

"No, but the convention is months away." Milton was quick to respond to end the conversation.

"So, then why is their discretionary spending red hot?" Randolph handed over additional accounting statements from his desk.

"Hmm," Milton actually stopped to consider that point. He hadn't seen much in the way of advertising or really much news about the DNC candidates. Of the three in the running, the majority of registered Democrats couldn't name the third and most couldn't pick the second out of a line-up.

"Because they are spending on advertising, for Nuthead!" Randolph finally got to the crux of his entire argument. He felt exhausted, mentally and physically, but by finally saying the words he felt that he could at last rest.

Randolph fell back into his seat as Milton eyed him.

"What?" Incredulity would be a subtle way to describe Milton's tone.

"The figures match, not 100%, but they are too close to be a coincidence." Randolph gestured to the papers in Milton's hands.

Now wanting to understand the argument, Milton rushed through the papers. "Nuthead is the antithesis of the DNC! This is the same thing that Hapless Wonder hinted at, but he had no figures to back it up!" The idea of the Democratic party funding a far-right fanatical Republican seemed to be ridiculous. The fact that the best candidate for the right had hinted at the connection, but was forced to bow-out after a sound beating in the polls, was almost tragic.

"Yeah, Nuthead is the worst thing to happen to the GOP, just like you said. It couldn't be going any better for the Dems than if they paid him." The 36-hour storm of investigation and activity had concluded for Randolph. He had put together the information and now he couldn't see any other way around the facts. It was true, Nuthead was just a long-con scam. "I don't know if they plan to have him bow out after all the other nominees drop out, or if they want him to go all the way through until November and then ruin his image, but they're paying him. We have a paper trail to show what they have been good at hiding up until now."

The pieces all connected for Milton, the reaction was incendiary.

"Holy shit!" Something fired up within Milton that he hadn't felt in some time. They were duping the American public, intentionally. They were harming the prospects of viable Republican candidates just to put their own candidates in a better position. This wasn't just a scandal; it was a rigged election. It was unheard of and went against every oath to state and country that he had ever heard of. Milton was mad at the DNC, he was mad at Nuthead, and he was instantaneously sick of the system. Pride, true and raw American pride, was what he was feeling. Milton couldn't believe it, but the dots were all connecting. The two political parties, that were supposed to stand for the ideals of democracy, help the people of the United States and other countries, were playing dodge-the-blame and spoil-the-soup with the Presidential election. Milton let out a deep and heated breath, the kind that is usually expelled from a lion that has been prodded and is more than angry enough to charge.

"Yeah, they're sitting back while Nuthead ruins what is left of the Grand Ole Party, and Nuthead is enough of a scrooge that he is going to take the money and enjoy the ride." Randolph felt disgusted as he said it.

"Holy shit!" Milton's mental queue was forming. *Who to validate this with? Who to ask for comment? Who to trust this with before print?*

"So, can I print any of this?" Randolph wanted to be published, but based on what he had uncovered, he just wanted the information out in the public. He knew that this information was more important than his own ambition. The Presidential election was being fixed, and it was plain as day. Would the American people even care though?

"Holy shit!" Milton wasn't much for exclamatory phrases, he just kept repeating his old standard.

"We're on deadline Milton, and I'd like to confirm the bribes paid to the polling committees too. No one is actually supporting Nuthead, but when a poll comes out and says that he is in the lead, everyone jumps onto that bandwagon." Randolph prodded Milton, wanting to get more than two words out of him.

"OK, kid you write it up and now," Milton scrambled for the original document he had glanced over. "Cut out the long metaphor, this is complicated enough as it is. I will cross reference to make sure we don't set off any landmines legally. But as long as the story breaks, that is what is important, people need to know."

"We haven't interviewed anyone, shouldn't we reach out for comment?" Randolph asked as he took the document back from Milton, unhappy about having to cut out his additional content, but happy to have made his point.

"Yes, that's what you usually do for me, it would be a conflict of interest in this case. Crap where is Tyler!" Milton stood on his feet and looked all around the newsroom. His first stop after finding Tyler would be to the Editor, with Randolph in tow.

"I'll text him," Randolph had his phone in his hand quickly, reflexively, like a good little Millennial.

"No, finish the story. Even if it sits for 24 hours we need to get this right. Nail 'em all to wall. Making a mockery of what should be the paragon of the democracy? Not on my watch!" Milton hadn't felt this fired up in a long time. He was happy to see that the kid took initiative, although he would have preferred to have been in the loop sooner so that they could have started to corroborate the facts that much earlier. Milton was ready to feel the thrill of uncovering a true scandal, a lie so big and splendid that it had to be true.

Milton texted Tyler and told him specifically to 'get his ass into work, right now!' and then began to get a list of contacts together. They would need additional first account quotes from people other than Randolph's granny and college roommate, but that should be easy enough to accomplish. Everyone knew someone in Florida. Iowa on the other hand was a bit less popular, but enough journalists were there to cover the caucus that it should be easy to scroll through Milton's list of contacts to find someone to verify that Nuthead's ads were all over the airwaves (even though nothing on TV ran through airwaves anymore).

Randolph edited and cut what he could, and made his point as obvious and clear as possible. He wanted the facts to speak for themselves and knew that readers could draw their own conclusion as to what it all meant. He made it pretty clear what he was trying to point out.

Within the hour Randolph was standing sheepishly behind Milton as his article was being read by the Editor, or as they called her, the Chief. A petite woman with sharp eyes and a work uniform of black pencil skirts and white blouses, she was a seasoned editor with a brassy New York accent.

The ultimate test of scrutiny was happening before Randolph's eyes. Either she would put the story down and begin to point out the flaws and inconsistencies in what was presented, or she would pick up her desk phone and call the legal department to confirm that the newspaper wouldn't be on the hook for libelous accusations. Randolph let out a sigh of relief when she did the latter. Milton turned and with a smirk gave the kid a wink. 'You passed.' Message received loud and clear, thought Randolph, who was busy trying to not smile like a baboon. *How could he be so happy when professional progression would always intersect with the exposure of a scandal or blatant lies to the American public?*

As he considered, for what felt like the millionth time that year, the longevity of his career, he could hear the Chief as she explained to the legal department the verity of his article. "They're spending alright, just staying quiet on their end and letting the GOP run themselves into the ground." She shook her head as she uttered the words, equally as disgusted as Milton and Randolph at the greed that was behind this scenario. The focus was so clearly on knocking out the opponent that the need for solid leadership had been lost. The need for a President had been replaced by the need to win, the need to be right, the need for power.

The next forty-eight hours were a whirlwind: involved parties were contacted for comment and given a respectable amount of time to respond; most, of course, gave no comment. The legal team vetted out the information and asked Randolph to remove a few areas that were speculative. They were poignant passages, but could have opened the door to potential lawsuits. The details regarding DNC employees receiving thick bonuses and then making large gifts to the employees of several polling organizations was wiped out. That would be a story for another time.

Milton aided where he could, holding firm to several points that Randolph wasn't sure whether to argue or not. The story was published and a fire-storm ensued, one that engulfed Nuthead's presidential campaign and left it in cinders. The Democrats tried their best to avoid the issue, but would eventually falter in the election not long after the DNC Chairwoman stepped down. The moderate candidate, and Milton's initial favorite to win, Hapless Wonder came back into the campaign. He went on to win the election, and eventually would balance the national debt during his tenure. Most immediately, campaign finance reform was at the forefront of the political agenda once again. This wasn't necessarily a bad thing, but it continued to detract from the real issues that every day Americans were facing.

Before the aftermath was fully realized, four gentleman played their nightly card game and toasted to Randolph's first headline and the incredible splash that it made. Randolph continued to give credit to Milton for his off-the-cuff remark that sparked the idea and his gusto to see the story published.

"So Randolph, are you going to keep uncovering political scandals for us?" Gregory prodded him, while also trying to divert attention from the cards laid during his bid.

Tyler smirked at the comment, he was envious of Randolph's success and wasn't hiding it well. Milton kept quiet and let Randolph enjoy the last bit of his glory, because once the clock struck midnight it would be a new day, and his article would, quite literally, be yesterday's news. Other papers were bound to latch on to try to find more dirt or try to disprove what Randolph had uncovered. Given the fact that all of Nuthead's ads had been pulled from every television network, Milton had absolutely no doubt as to the validity of Randolph's claim.

The game ended. Tyler and Gregory once again were on the losing end. This time, instead of beers Milton requested a bottle of champagne to toast Randolph. Gregory agreed, Tyler muttered, and they both went out into the dark night to fetch the victors' spoils.

"They should really ask us to play another game, they're both terrible Bridge players," Randolph commented and he picked up the cards and began to shuffle.

Rifle, bridge.
Rifle, bridge.
Rifle, bridge.

"Eh, I'm pretty good at almost every card game. I've learned that the best way to crack a good witness is to play a few hands of cards first. It loosens them up, makes them feel cozy."

"Well, I will have to keep that in mind," Randolph savored the advice from his mentor, although he was unsure as to when he would use it.

"So, what is your next story kid? If you don't put together another one fast, and a good one, then you'll be a one-hit wonder around here."

Randolph nodded considering Milton's words.

Rifle, bridge.

Rifle, bridge.

"But you also don't want to spit out a story that isn't credible either. I've seen a lot of young fellas like yourself try to prove themselves after a big piece by coming out with another great one right afterwards, only to have it fall flat, or worse be discredited." Milton was gesturing with his hands, speaking from his years of experience in seeing journalists come and go. Randolph nodded, lost in thought, his mind off somewhere on another planet, or at least another space and time.

"So?" Milton was trying to prompt a reply.

"So, I think I'm not cut out for the political beat. I've wanted to be this for so long, to be a younger version of you," Randolph admitted what had been gnawing at him openly and without hesitation. "I've been feeling myself become more and more frustrated with the system. I've never been that kind of person that was 'against the Man,' but I can feel it, deep down, that my views are shifting and they are shifting because of this job."

Milton remained un-phased by Randolph's comments of adoration and disillusion. "If this job didn't change you, then you wouldn't be doing it correctly."

Randolph nodded and accepted Milton's words. But he had more to say, to get off of his chest. It was all boiling up from the excitement of the day, receiving so much praise over uncovering such a horrible truth.

"I just feel like this isn't what we want everyone to think it is. We're not much better than the tabloids. People think that we're so prestigious and special because it is the politicians we are providing gossip about. That the political gossip is 'real news'. Real news is when a dictator starves his own citizens and the people of the world ignore it because it would be too uncomfortable to admit that our everyday luxury is expendable. Real news is when a natural disaster wipes out a village, but the people are so resilient that they begin to rebuild the next day. This," Randolph picked up the front page of that day's paper, his headline and name above the fold: *The Joker: How a Long-Con Fixed the 2016 Election!* "This is a score update on a game, a new strategy being employed in a no-win scenario. This isn't news, this is fodder."

Randolph had finally said the words that had been itching to get out of his mind all day. He wanted to respond to each 'well done' and 'congratulations' with a 'for what?' He didn't feel that his work merited much celebration or excitement, because he knew that the next day, or the next week, some other scheme would be hatched. It was just a never-ending tennis game where both sides only gained a brief advantage, but couldn't win the point. Randolph was beginning to think that politicians should be featured on ESPN instead of CNN; they were all just playing their constituents anyways. Playing with their livelihoods, entertaining them with yelling and finger-wagging. They weren't much different from the animated coaches on the sidelines throwing their hats or their chairs.

Randolph saw it all for what it was, a giant game. Wasn't that the latest buzz word- gamification? They 'gamified' learning, they 'gamified' diets, and finally, they had 'gamified' politics. No substance behind the outcome, just a machine churning out more problems to keep the crooks in Washington in demand.

Milton could sense that Randolph had reached a tipping point. He knew that there was a decision on the horizon. Randolph would refuse to accept the reality of the world that he lived in, which would plague each job he had; or he would accept that ideals are meant to be shattered and continue to work hard to expose the truth in any given situation. Milton had made his decision long ago, when people were merely skeptical. But now, there was an omnipresent apathy upon the people.

Milton sighed and carefully expressed what wisdom he had to Randolph, whose eyes were pleading for advice. "You can't make everyone honest and you can't make every person care. You have to accept that coming in. We all hope that one story, one piece of information could wake everyone up out of the trance they are all in."

Randolph nodded, "Yes!" He was almost pleading for that option to be viable.

"But that is a fairy tale," Milton gestured with his hand to demonstrate how fleeting that concept was. "Just as much as Cinderella is a story. All we can do is try. We present the facts; we provide the information that we know the people should care about. And occasionally we give them the crap that they just want to see." Milton gestured behind him at his computer screen, now locked, but behind the cheery screensaver was a human-interest story. Fluff, complete fluff, but he knew it would please the masses.

"So that's it? Expose the truth, hope something good comes from it, and then just-?" Randolph paused. "What? Just move on?"

"Yep," Milton refocused on the pile of pretzel sticks in front of him. He was hungry and his attention span started to fade.

Randolph was truly stumbling for words. He couldn't just let the topic go. "But,-" Randolph was really grasping to continue his thought, but his best efforts were failing him.

"But, didn't this story shatter the last façade of American Democracy?" Randolph looked down at the newspaper in his hands, now it felt flimsy, where only an hour ago it felt solid and important.

"It's always been a façade. American disillusionment is

at an all-time high. Those intelligent enough to understand see it as the 'same ole, same ole', and those who are dense enough to still be shocked are too gullible to realize that they have actually been duped every single time." Milton stopped to make sure he didn't hurt the kid's feelings. "What you uncovered matters."

Milton looked across to Randolph to make sure the kid looked up and made eye contact with him. After a few seconds he did.

"This story matters. Don't for a second think that this isn't important. But, remember that tomorrow there will be another scandal that needs to be found, and another politician that has gone crooked. There isn't an end to this."

"How can you live with that? How can you accept it?" Randolph's idealism was rearing its polished and pretty head again.

"Well, it provides job security, so I guess I couldn't make a living without it." Milton smiled and his humorous attempt to end the conversation worked.

Randolph smirked and nodded his head. "I guess that isn't so bad then."

Tyler and Gregory returned with the champagne. Into their mugs it was poured and a final toast was given to Randolph. "Here's to taking down Nuthead! Who are you going after next?" Gregory offered.

"Hmm, well Pierrot has been a little too quiet lately. Maybe he is up to something," Randolph responded with an air of mystery. He drank the champagne and slipped into the easy enjoyment of camaraderie.

"He's a French mime, he's supposed to be quiet." Milton jostled Randolph and the group finished their drink, played the next round of Bridge, and departed the building after their work was done. In the cold walk home Randolph recalled the joy of the day, his copy of the paper tucked securely under his arm. Somewhere in between his subway stop and his cramped apartment, the hour stuck midnight. With a new day the game was reset. In the cool air of that night, came the moment when Randolph would decide if he would let that headline tucked under his arm become his only accomplishment or a galvanizing first of many. He mulled over the sophistication of the delicate and elaborate game that the candidates and pundits played where only they could win. Randolph decided in that moment the he would beat them all at their own game. He would master it and turn them on their heads.

DOLLY

The static nature of our game is solved,
Wins and Losses divided equal between both teams.
But that was always the thing about you and California,
You only ever dealt in dreams.

So I'm headed to my bright orange horizon,
And if I find the time when I get there
I'll learn how to write down the word "forgiveness"
And send it to you; but you'll act like you don't even care.

<u>Sunday</u>

It was a calm and beautiful morning in California. The gulls were sounding off above the churning water of the Pacific; flapping, gliding, diving and, coasting on the air above the soft and unending waves of Malibu. The calm and soothing sounds of the ocean filtered into the state-of-the-art mansion sitting on this prime piece of real-estate. The evolutionary processes taking place not twenty feet away were unnoticed, as they often are. It is ironic because the beating of the water against the sand, the slow process by which sediment is pulled out into the sea, and then pushed back to begin the process again, is a showcase of one the most understood truths of this planet: time reveals all things.

That morning was no different. A secret, but not even one that was intentionally being hidden, had resurfaced. A slender and vivacious blonde bounced up the beach and headed for the third deck past the jetty. She minded the wooden stairs with grace and grabbed the towel she had set out on the patio bar. After drying off the surf, sand, and sweat from her morning swim and run, she pulled her hair out of its tie and shook her long golden locks free.

The sliding door back into the house was still ajar; this had allowed the sounds of the morning into the house. Of course, it also let the air-conditioning escape, which was wasteful, but they could afford it. Or more precisely, her much older beaux could afford it. She smiled and tiptoed into the house, her feet silently pressing against the cool granite flooring. Her post work-out routine would allow her body temperature to return to normal and keep her metabolism buzzing all day.

Immediately, she noticed that something was amiss. The man who was 20 years her senior, who was usually still asleep at this early hour, was not only awake, but was moving with a precision and speed that she thought impossible for a man of his size and age. She was startled to find him moving about the beach house during her quiet time.

"Hey Jay, you're up early!" She tried to sound excited and happy about this fact, as though she might enjoy a few extra hours with him. But this was her "me-time" and she liked to have a few hours in the morning to herself. She put on her big smile, but was immediately nervous that she had on no make-up. She worried that if Jay noticed this, he may soon start to look for an even younger and more gorgeous girl to have on his arm.

"Hey babe," he waved her off. She was the most recent in a string of girlfriends. She could have been any one of them to Jay that morning, but she was Helen Graham. If she had quizzed him as to her name at that very moment, Jay likely would not have answered correctly. He was so focused and intent on whatever it was that he was doing. Jay had his laptop fired up and was frantically typing into his iPhone.

Jay was a large fellow with poor posture. His figure resembled that of a mound of laundry, or a happy Buddha figurine, as he leaned into his laptop screen. He most likely needed reading glasses. Helen didn't recall him mentioning any morning meetings, especially on a Sunday. But she shrugged her shoulders and pressed on; she was used to how easily he dismissed her.

"The surf this morning was great! Do you want me to make you some pancakes?" She wasn't planning to alter her routine, but she was willing to accommodate. Helen did her exercise, made herself a healthy breakfast, and then would shower before heading out to meet up with her girlfriends for an afternoon of shopping and dining. She had to at least offer to include Jay in her routine; that was the polite thing to do. Especially considering that it was his house and his food that she was living in for free, or almost free.

"No, I'm fine." Jay was short and to the point. It was clear that he didn't want to talk. Helen rolled her eyes, knowing that he couldn't see her, and proceeded to the kitchen to prepare her flax-seed pancakes with an avocado and seaweed shake. She was on a strict diet before her audition, which was made possible by Jay. Being the arm-candy of the second most powerful man in Hollywood had its perks and she was aware of the small price she paid each evening to be the beneficiary of these advantages.

Helen moved about the kitchen while keeping a close eye on Jay; his behavior that morning was completely out of the ordinary. She usually didn't ask him about his work. Ryan James Karkowitz, known to all as Jay, was the Chief Operating Officer at Criss Entertainment Holdings. What was there for Helen to know? He spent most of his afternoons hanging around with his long-time best friend who also happened to be his boss: The Joseph Criss. She knew that Jay had meetings, but usually that meant a golf game or lunch with some big-time guys. It was the typical L.A. boy's club; she didn't think he actually did much work. She certainly didn't think he ever worked much on weekdays, let alone the weekend. Jay was not a mysterious man, but that morning Helen was puzzled by him: his behavior, his demeanor, his movements. He was like a stranger to her.

As she started up the blender, she saw Jay pick up the iPhone, before it even rang, and began to ask rapid-fire questions to the person who had been unfortunate enough to call him.

"OK, and you have a name? - Great, now get me everything you can, I want all the details and all the dirt. - No, I don't want your opinion. If I did I would ask for it! - Good, now that we have that clear, can you send me a run-down of how far the damage has spread? Are we just on MSNBC and CNN or have we spread into the regular news programs and – well, why didn't you say so sooner. Don't call me back until you have some answers. We need to kill this story now!" He slammed the phone down on the kitchen table where he had set up his mini-crisis center. Jay was sweating, which usually would have elated Helen to see him finally exerting himself and maybe even working out. But this was not a healthy sweat by any means. His face was getting red; she began to worry that he might have an episode of some kind from high blood pressure or whatever it is that men of his age have to worry about.

"Is everything okay, honey?" Timid, and not wanting to invoke the same anger that was just unleashed on an employee, Helen hoped to sooth her gentle giant.

"Yeah, it's fine," Jay replied, trying his best not to snap at her by adding a smile and quickly redirecting his attention. He unplugged his laptop and walked over to the large sofa that was positioned in front of the fireplace. Over the mantle was a large flat-screen TV. Jay had once told her that this model wasn't even for sale yet in the US, but that he and Joseph had been given a free version because of their connections with the Japanese manufacturer.

Jay turned on the TV and began to flip through the channels quickly. Jay had never been much of a TV person; she had rarely seen him use the thing expect for when he was screening films prior to submitting his ballot for the Academy Awards. Helen returned to her pancakes, which were about done and decided to make up a plate for Jay. Whether he had asked or not, she knew he would need to eat. She was also secretly hoping that some food might put him in a better mood. He didn't get to be 300 pounds by avoiding food.

Jay had stopped flipping through the channels and settled on some political talk show. Now Helen knew something peculiar had to be going on. Jay was about as knowledgeable on politics as the next guy, which was, not very knowledgeable at all. He thought that ISIS was the name of a new model/actress and that soldiers were primarily top material for action films. He couldn't even name the Vice President if quizzed. *0 for 2 this morning Jay,* Helen thought to herself.

On the television, there was a panel of people going back and forth in a round table style debate. They were discussing the newest Supreme Court Justice, who had only been appointed recently. Helen only knew this because one of her friends was a super feminist and talked her ear off about this woman for hours when she was being appointed, or voted on, or whatever the process was. For as much as she didn't really care about women's lib, wasn't that their parent's thing anyway? Helen was happy to see that this judge, or justice, was at least pretty. They would make a good movie about her one day; maybe. Helen could only hope that Jay would help option it and maybe squeeze her into the cast.

As Helen was putting the final touches on the plates and set a small container of syrup and cinnamon butter on a serving tray, Jay's iPhone began to ring. He had left it on the kitchen table and looked startled to see how far away it was from him, across the room. Helen quickly walked over to the table, and scooped it up, handing it over to Jay quickly. His hand was already outstretched, reaching for it and clamping his hands as though he was a child indicating that he needed his toy immediately.

He answered it in a split second once the phone was in-hand and slouched back into the couch.

"Hey man- Yeah I'm watching it now, I will say that so far we seem safe, they are keeping the focus on the Court, no mention of our ca- What? – Look, I know that we have a lot to handle now, but they are already losing steam, the story will die out in a few days- Joseph you need to calm down…"

She could tell that this was bad. Jay had been worked up, but now he was the one who was trying to calm down Joseph. She knew right away that Joseph was Joseph Criss. She had never seen him worked up either. Helen knew that he and Jay had started Criss Entertainment together, a few years out of college and moved the company to L.A. from New York early on. They were best friends living the dream of running a successful company. In the past year, the company had pursued some lawsuit about taxes, but that had been going on for a while. *Was this commotion that morning connected to the case?*

Jay was silent on the phone and intently watching as the photo on the screen of the polished female: the new Justice, Hertzfeld or something, was replaced by an older black-and-white photo. Helen recognized Joseph in the older photo right away, who could miss him? Then she noticed immediately to his left was the Justice, a much, much younger version of the woman whose image had just been displayed.

Helen stopped and began to listen intently to the conversation that the panelists on the show were having.

"I understand the point that you are making, and maybe the end result will be that she recuses herself from this case, but that is only if she feels that she can't be impartial," a woman with a man's haircut began to elaborate before she was cut off by a pasty-faced fat man.

"How could she not be impartial, she practically helped found the company. She used to sit on the board!"

"Well it's clear that she didn't get this far in her career without being able to be impartial on cases where she might have personal feelings." A third panelist had chimed in. This was a young man, with a sharp tone, millennial attitude, and a Blackberry in hand while on camera.

"This could be another Sandy Day bemoaning that the election was called and then stepping up to write a pivotal decision in the 2000 Bush v. Gore case." Pasty face made a reference that the other panelists understood, but it was lost on his audience in Malibu.

"That's not even close to this. And quite frankly, I doubt we would even be having this discussion if Hertzfeld-Doll was a man. Now-a-days many successful men, and women, are asked to sit on the board of companies and when they no longer have the capacity, or interest, they leave the board. That's what happened here almost three decades ago." The female with the man's haircut made a solid point. Helen found herself nodding in agreement absentmindedly, she didn't even know the issue at hand. *Very persuasive,* thought Helen.

"But this wasn't a cut and dry case of sitting on the board then leaving. She was the person who filed the original incorporation paperwork. She was a classmate of both Criss and Karkowitz. She had as much to do with the founding of this company as any of the other founding members. We don't know how involved she was. Maybe it was a simple case of an old classmate helping with a start-up, although we wouldn't have used that term in the late 80s. But it could be as complicated as Herzfeld-Doll knowing in a legal and business sense 'where the bodies are buried'." The younger Blackberry wielding male came back this time.

Jay had fidgeted at the mention of his name, a motion that did not go unnoticed by his girlfriend. *What kind of trouble are Jay and Joseph into?*

"So then, she doesn't handle this case, that's easy. End of story. There is no risk of her being impartial if she doesn't preside." The original female panelist responded. Jay nodded adamantly, clearly in support of her conclusion.

"Although it will increase the likelihood of a split vote," the smug moderator with a comb-over and bow-tie snuck in a brief sentence before he was interrupted.

"Not so fast, the timing of this case always seemed off to me. I wonder if Criss didn't secretly hope that this was never found out and tried to slide it in as one of the first cases that his old friend could preside over." Pasty face was bringing on the negativity. The socialite girlfriend of Jay Karkowitz would have never known how entertaining these passive-aggressive political shows could be; Helen was hooked.

"Now that is entirely speculation. This seems like a pure coincidence." The moderator finally interjected between the verbal catfight breaking out between the other commentators.

"And what if this story from Entertainment Weekly never surfaced, would she have stepped down on her own?" Pasty-face added his latest question. Helen couldn't help but notice how greasy his receding hairline was. This man needed to fire his political advisors and hire a stylist, quickly. Although no amount of clothes and product could hide the doughy jowls of the aging politician.

"Well, we'll never know now." The woman with the masculine hairdo responded.

Jay began to tense yet again as he watched the dialog. It appeared that Joseph had stopped talking as well; perhaps they were both listening to the show. They had both been called out already in the few minutes that they were watching.

"Going back to the point you were making earlier, yes we may not be having this conversation if Hertzfeld was a man, and mainly because there wouldn't be, well, other questions raised." The moderator was trying to stoke the coals a bit with this comment, it worked.

"What do you mean other questions?" Masculine hairdo seemed to be offended.

"Criss' reputation is known-" The younger man with the checkered button down and unfortunate complexion added to the comment from the moderator, gesturing with his Blackberry. Was the implication romantic? Helen wondered.

"I can't believe I'm hearing any of this. Are you really

about to slander a sitting Supreme Court Justice merely because she is a female who used to go to the same Ivy League school as Joseph Criss? I have two words for you: lawyer up." Masculine hairdo made a great point. Jay's girlfriend was connecting the dots. Helen had clearly picked a side in this argument, although she didn't know all of the details, but it seemed like this new Justice was getting crapped all over for no good reason. Joseph was a lothario but as far as she knew, he tended to prefer women much younger, even younger than her. Always blonde, slender, 24 or 25. They were all pretty sharp too, she had been on several double dates with Jay and Joseph. Although Jay had kept her around much longer than any of Joseph's girls.

The moderator of the show jumped in and announced that it was time for a commercial. Helen could hear what Joseph was telling Jay loud and clear, he was yelling through the phone. "I don't care what you have to do, Jay, or who you have to pay off, you kill this thing now! We have to save Dolly! I won't accept this!!"

<u>Monday</u>

She sat quietly at her desk, timid to start the workday. No pen in hand, no blank paper in front of her, she was poised and postured. The air in her office was strangely perfumed in that she had no familiarity with the scent, but it was sweet and welcoming. Katherine assumed it was left by one of the many chemicals utilized by the night cleaning crew. She inhaled deeply and let the aroma in through her perfectly round nose that was the effort of generations of Nordic and European breeding. She let the air fill the upper part of her lungs and force her torso to extend outward, making her loose white silk blouse tighten and then release.

Her lithe, long fingers were gently pressed to the carved edges of her refined hardwood desk. The once bright wood paneling that surrounded her was now cool and bland. But the historic value of the décor made her aesthetic unease subside. It had only been a month since she had moved into her office and in that time she managed to artfully place her degrees on the walls, arrange her desk, and meet with her colleagues; who just also happened to be her career idols. She brushed up on her anthology of legal references while dusting them off and arranging them on her bookshelves. Everything was put into place just as it should be ordered.

Her family photos were all facing her, on one end a recent photo of her with her husband, Ron, and their family dog, a dachshund named Beans. On the other end of her desk was a photo of her and Ron with their two children, Martha and Abigail, taken on a family trip to Mount Rushmore in the late nineties. For such an outwardly serious and reserved person, Katherine delighted in her candid and smiling picture, and for the goofy family trip photo that faced her. They reminded her to smile and not be so serious. On particularly difficult days in the office, she would focus on Abigail with her multitude of freckles and bobbed messy hair and the way she was stretching the edges of her mouth open and sticking her tongue out at the photographer.

Katherine had been focusing on that picture more and more since the whole hubbub boiled up the previous week. Not only because of the number of difficult days that were piling up, but because the joking and casual Abigail, forever 9 in that photo, looked almost identical to Katherine at that same age. Skinny, but lanky, wearing clothes that were clearly too big because she was uncomfortable with her body. Abigail took after her mother: she had thick and matted dusty blonde hair, a passion for American History and the law, and an awkward manner of remaining silent and observing before speaking succinctly and decidedly. Mother and daughter were not very different at all. Martha was like Ron and loved to spend time hiking, and biking, and all manner of rugged outdoor activities. Martha had spent most of that trip running ahead of the rest of the family and calling after them to catch up to her on the trail.

The proud mother smiled and made a mental note to call both of her daughter's within the week to catch-up with them. They had likely tried to phone over the weekend when their mother's name was all over the news, but kind and practical Ron had disconnected the land-line and locked their cell phones in his desk drawer. Katherine jotted down a reminder on a sticky-note and her latest morning distraction ended. She focused on her surroundings yet again: her office and her to-do list for the day, that wasn't going anywhere by dwelling on the fond memories of the past. Her recent focus on the troubles at hand didn't help either.

Katherine had a calm air about her as she took on her latest challenge. However, the new role and reaching the pinnacle of her career was quickly shadowed by the media scandal that had suddenly stirred up over the most inane bit of old gossip. She rolled her eyes thinking of how utterly ridiculous the news media had become. She had been raised in a time when the evening news anchors were all well-educated and focused on the serious events of the day like war, nuclear fall-out, and human rights.

She tried to shake the thoughts out of her mind, but it was a futile task. She even motioned her head slightly as though it was something she could actually shake out; that her worries would somehow dislodge and come spilling out of her left ear. Katherine looked ahead and decided that she needed to get to work.

She began by reviewing the briefs that had been gathering on her desk. The docket for the upcoming term would be tame, Katherine smiled slightly at the thought. The judicial sessions that were predicted to be the most inconsequential had often been the most notorious. A true scholar, she had studied the law and the influence of the Court for decades.

Katherine grabbed the thick brief on the top of her pile and leaned back. The burgundy leather chair creaked as she settled into it. This partially worried her that it could give out at any moment. That would be the worst part of her bad extended weekend: breaking a chair with her aging rear-end in one of the most historic and respected establishments in western civilization. She skimmed the introduction to the brief, she could easily identify that her most senior clerk had written the draft by the style and wording. She pursed her lips as she reviewed the heart of the matter, a commerce clause case. What to the lay-person might be the most odious bit of law, truly fascinated Katherine. *This will be an interesting one, indeed.* She smiled and felt the gears in her brain begin to whir as she read on through the rest of the document.

Katherine spent the rest of the morning making notes and indexing the relevant case law. She filled several pages of her note pad with her thoughts and questions, put the brief aside on the far end of her desk, the "done" pile, and decided it was time for lunch. Katherine was dreading a trip to the cafeteria. She would be expected to socialize and the chit-chat would only be a thin veil for what she assumed was on everyone's mind. As most humans do, she tended to assume that her most personal turmoil was painted all over her face and that it was most certainly on the top of everyone's mind. Katherine reminded herself that she was being ridiculous. She steadied herself by thinking of the comforting words offered by her husband. Ron had agreed that the recent media spotlight was laughable. He was always able to cut right to the heart of the matter.

Just that morning, he had rubbed her shoulders while

she agonized over the morning paper and reminded her that in the long run, history would remember what was ahead of her, not behind her. Katherine smiled at that recent memory as she meandered down the long marbled hallways to the staircase.

She would always remember her first days at the Court decades earlier and how she made an effort to love every square inch of it, including the staircase. She thought back on the time when she clerked for Souter.

Katherine sought to be a Souter, an enigmatic and dignified Justice. She was not off to a good start. Katherine pranced down the stairs. She had never lost her natural bounce and balance. She had always quickly jotted down any case of stairs, whether she was in a rush or not. It was just her habit. She was proud that age had not yet snuck into her joints, they were not yet stiff with ineptitude. There had been one misstep, when she had been clerking and Souter had wanted an updated brief on a short deadline. Katherine, back then everyone called her Katie, surprisingly didn't remember the exact case, but she remembered slipping when her toe narrowly missed the step underneath her. This small trip-up had caused papers to fly out everywhere. Needless to say the documents arrived later than originally planned.

Katherine tried to slow her pace a bit as she recalled that earlier spill, but she was still descending the staircase rather quickly. Her soft brown leather shoes hurriedly plucked along the white and gray swirls on the marble below her and made a soft tap-tap-tap as she passed each step. Having decided to push aside her concerns and focus on a positive outcome for the day, her hunger quickly took control of her motor functions. She arrived at the entrance to the cafeteria promptly. The basement cafeteria was relatively empty, which was lucky for Katherine. She had imagined it as a constant bustling of lawyers, lobbyists, and politicians when she was a young woman. Her first month as a clerk several decades ago had proven her wrong, and it appeared that time had not changed much in terms of the moderate to light use of the common dining space.

What she had once imagined as the busy and clique-controlled cafeteria that she had seen in her high school days was really an empty menagerie of today's specials. During the academic year there was the occasional field trip, at which point most of the staff tried to avoid the cafeteria. It wasn't that educating the nation's future wasn't of interest to everyone in the building. However, when the next leaders of the free world were still in grade school, lunch-time was somewhat akin to a yelling and screaming circus. The voices of the delighted young children would usually echo lightly through the halls and signal everyone to order lunch to be delivered to their offices.

Seeing as it was only early August, the school tours wouldn't start for at least another month. Katherine waved politely to one of the chefs behind the salad station and stood pondering all of the options. The clam chowder, advertised as the daily special on the main chalkboard by the stack of food trays, would be her back-up option if nothing else caught her attention. Katherine tried her best to bring a packed lunch every day during her career, but in the last month she noticed that she had developed a habit of treating herself to a bought-lunch almost daily. After a month of sampling all of the available entrees and sides, her palate was beginning to tire of the rotation and she knew that she would likely prepare her own lunches again shortly. *If it's something that I find to be dull, why pay for it every day?*

Katherine identified one of the available pastas of the day and considered a hearty helping with tomato sauce and a breadstick. Just like any woman, when she was stressed or frustrated, carbohydrates were always there for comfort. Reliable and delicious, they never let her down. But, she decided against it. After weighing the options, she determined that a bottle of water and a chicken sandwich would be best.

She made her way across the recently cleaned and waxed white linoleum floor and greeted the woman at the cash register with a smile. Today it was Marjorie that was working. She was short and aging, Katherine estimated that Marjorie should have already been collecting social security, but would never dare to ask.

Marjorie was a sweet old woman who squinted through her thick eye-glasses as she began to punch in Katherine's lunch order into the electronic monitor in front of her. Marjorie searched for the proper entry "Entrée- Sandwich" and pressed hard onto the screen until the tip of her index finger was at a 45-degree angle with the rest of her finger, her fingertip blanching white against her pink skin. The computer recognized her entry and Marjorie let out a small smile and set off to find the water bottle entry in the system. Katherine smiled patiently, knowing that Marjorie was trying as hard as she could. Fortunately, there was no line and, from the looks of it, only two other people in the vicinity. One was a male clerk on break in the far corner reading a novel while hunched over a club sandwich. The other was a young woman who was scanning through some information of her smart phone while sipping on a coffee.

Marjorie had completed the order and asked Katherine for $10.75 for her lunch. Katherine handed over her bright red check card; a small homage to the Philadelphia Phillies that she paid an extra few dollars for when she updated her bank account a few years back. Marjorie swiped the card effortlessly, as though rheumatism had yet to spoil her wrists, and Katherine pocketed the card. Transaction completed. Katherine's stomach was appreciative.

After grabbing a set of utensils from the plastic aerated bins on the condiment bar by the entrance to the cafeteria, Katherine walked over to an empty table in the far back corner. There was an abundance of seating options given that there were only two other people there at the time. However, she was struck by the sudden phenomenon that washes over Americans when they find themselves in the same common space as strangers. They disperse. The seats that were right up front were far too close to the young girl with the coffee. Seats that were closest to the exit were too close to the young man reading the novel. Even though she could have found a seat at least 10 feet away from either of them, seeing that there was an unclaimed corner 30 feet away, she opted for the least socially uncomfortable spot. Seated in the far back corner of the cafeteria, the entrance was obscured by the heaters and trays of food on display.

Katherine placed a napkin on her lap, twisted the thin plastic cap on her water bottle and took a quick, cool sip. She looked out the window on her left at the dirty, hollowed-out cement alcove that had captured twigs and leaves from trees that were some way away, but that had been carried there by an errant breeze. The cafeteria was technically located below ground, but somehow managed to still accommodate windows at the ceiling level. There was a soft warm patch of blue sky visible just above the ground level, and seeing the clear sky from this far beneath the ground made her smile.

Katherine was grateful that there were no colleagues to smile at her shyly. They would have been polite, but their overly nice gestures would still let her know that her past choices were being scrutinized. Even though she did nothing wrong, she felt as though she was tied to a stake at a witch-hunt.

She couldn't blame her fellow Justices if they had been there and given her such a look; after all, they were judges by profession. *How could they not sit and judge her?* She pushed the thoughts from her mind once again and found it was much easier to do than it had been the day before. It was getting easier to put her tough skin back on, and focus on what she needed to in that moment. Katherine began to eat. She was glad to feel that she was making progress at salvaging a normal day. She enjoyed the brief reprieve for a few moments, until there was a loud whining sound of metal scratching linoleum that caused her to jerk her head up and see what was coming her way.

The Previous Wednesday

The connection between a sitting Supreme Court Justice and the CEO and Founder of Criss Entertainment Holdings only became a story in the news media because of the deep-digging of an ambitious junior reporter at Entertainment Weekly. With the latest ruling in the matter of Criss Entertainment Holdings, LLC v State of California likely to face a final appeal and appear in front of the Supreme Court, Justin Ames, who was two years out of UC Berkley and eager to make a name for himself in Los Angeles, was digging through legal textbooks and publicly released documents dating back to the incorporation of the company in 1986.

Ames was going bleary-eyed on the details of the company and the case itself. He had minored in Constitutional Law in college, meaning he took three courses on the history of the American legal system and an additional elective in moot court. His initial ambition to be a lawyer when he entered college eventually evolved into a desire to be a hard-hitting reporter. He pictured himself exposing the failings of the modern legal system and perhaps traveling to underdeveloped countries to report on atrocities against basic human rights. In spite of his ambition, efforts, and hours working away at The Daily Californian, he was left without job prospects when he graduated in 2014 and worked his way down the California coast until he arrived in Los Angeles. Desperate for a job writing anything, Ames was about to accept an offer as a copywriter in the marketing department of a weight-loss supplement manufacturer when he got a lead on a job at *Entertainment Weekly*.

Ames put on his most ambitious face for the interview and fumbled his way through questions about the latest celebrity relationship "news" and style trends. Finally, he was able to impress his editor, Bruce Unger, with obscure movie and music knowledge. Ames salvaged the interview and somehow managed to get an offer. He celebrated with the few friends he had found in Hollywood and toasted to the start of his career. Although, Ames could feel something nagging at his soul as he began the new job. Would he be less of a sell-out by writing ads for weight loss supplements than by writing up the latest news on J. Law's love life or Kim Kardashian's latest perfume? But he smiled through it.

Now was his chance to shine. The second that whispers began to circulate that Criss Entertainment was looking to re-incorporate in Ireland because of some obscure tax loophole in order to avoid hefty payments to the U.S. government, Ames walked right up to his editor and requested the story. "Tax exemptions? Come on Ames, at most this will be a paragraph in the back of our next issue." Unger wasn't overly excited about the pitch. Ames persisted, and lucky for him, he had already claimed his stake on what could be his first huge story.

A few weeks after the announcement was made, the bars in town were lit up with chatter of whether jobs would be lost and what the local impact to the community would be if the company had to move because of the status change. Ames wrote up another piece and his editor held it for a few weeks before he had an empty space to fill. Unger made it clear to Ames that luck was the only reason it was being published and to focus on the stories that would capture the attention of their readers. "Need I remind you that you are not working for *The Economist*, Ames?"

Two months later, the United States government and the IRS sent a notarized letter to Joseph Criss, CEO and founder of Criss Entertainment Holdings. This letter detailed their intention to levy taxes against the company in spite of the planned relocation, given the company's origins. Whether Criss received the letter himself or had the details explained to him by his legal team, he went on a media rampage. He held press conferences and burned the letter on live television. It quickly became such an iconic image to see him stare his crystalline green eyes into the camera directly in front of him and say, "Sam, you're one funny Uncle that I'd like to get away from!" The media ate it up and Ames was poised to capitalize on this moment. He heard rumors that James Marsden was already in talks to portray Criss in the movie that was sure to be optioned the second the matter was resolved.

Criss was known in Hollywood for two things: being a lothario and being a visionary in terms of developing the movie industry. He started Criss Entertainment in his early twenties and grew it from a small time ad production studio to a TV and movie powerhouse. Every year he topped the Forbes list of most influential people. He was generous with his money, not only giving to the charities that made requests upon him, but also lavishing his latest lovers with extravagant trinkets.

It was clear the guy didn't need money to win the ladies over, nor did he need the cologne of success and power. Criss was charming, funny, and he looked good playing football on the beach when he visited a film set. One day he interrupted production for over two hours to play a pick-up game with George Clooney, Matt Damon, Brad Pitt and the crew. Though he was in his late fifties, Criss was what Ames had heard several females call "a silver fox." His smile was ridiculously white, and every photo Ames could find of him dating back to the founding of the company proved he had always looked that good. The only way he could tell the difference between current photos and those from the archive were the poor quality of the older photos and the light salt and pepper framing Criss' face in current pictures.

Ames knew that the charismatic CEO would help to sell the story, but he first had to piece all of the details together. A full year after his first small write-up was penned, he was busy working on the grand article. Ames stretched and yawned in his chair. The office was empty and Ames rejoiced in the feeling of being a true journalist as he burned the midnight oil. He reviewed his notes again to help keep all of the details clear. He didn't want to write up a puff piece on why Criss was so great and why he should win his case based on his looks or philanthropic achievements. Ames wanted to base his argument on the law.

It was in that late-night, caffeine fueled, fast-food bloated evening, when the rest of the young and ambitious in L.A. were at the clubs, that Ames was hunched over his small desk trying to find the angle for his story. Usually his desk was clean, he didn't need much paperwork in order to write up whether Justin Bieber was dating or just going to dinner with another ingénue. This wasn't his usual story though. Ames had boxes of archival copies sent over to the office and had built himself a wall of documents to pour through to find the angle he needed. His editor wasn't pleased, but Ames was dedicated.

As one day bled into the next, and his lower back started to ache from the rolling chair with no lumbar support, and his eyes started to wince from dehydration, Ames picked up one last folder for the evening. He downed the last of the Coke can that was on his desk, crushed it, and threw it toward the recycle bin a few feet away. He missed. Fortunately, no one saw. Ames rushed to pick it up and throw it away properly and then returned to his chair.

The next folder up was from a cocktail party. The date listed 1988, but the party itself was on New Year's Eve, December 1987. The folder contents were seemingly simple, containing receipts and invoices from vendors. A final invitation with engraved lettering was also included. Ames wondered why a company would keep such mundane details after decades. It was likely that no one had gone through the documents since they passed the audit threshold of seven years and were long forgotten. Ames shook his head and dug on. He was hoping that in the long forgotten files there would be some bit of information that would keep his story going. He gave the invitation list a once over and then saw a few clippings from society pages with photos of guests at the party.

The first was one of Jay Karkowitz, Criss' Chief Operating Officer, college roommate, and overall best friend and confidant. Jay was pictured in a dapper tuxedo, clearly he had put on a few pounds since the late 80s. Jay was now more or less an unseen, but still supremely powerful fixture in the Criss organization. Next to Karkowitz were some of the other board members in very dated attire. The shoulder pads on the women's evening gowns were a dead give-away to the decade.

Ames picked up the next clipping and it was like a gear that had been off-pace finally got in-step with a cog in his brain. He double checked the caption to confirm and then raced through the papers to read through the invitation list again. The name that he had glanced over, the one that sounded familiar, now came to life in his mind. Ames was energized and started typing away. He had found the angle for his article and already had the perfect picture for the front cover of the next issue.

<u>Monday</u>

That's how quick it can take in the twenty-first century to unravel years of professional ascension and the intellectual pursuit of the law. In all of the excitement that Ames had coursing through his veins by getting to pen his first big story, he forgot that he was simultaneously ruining the reputation of the newly appointed Supreme Court Justice Katherine Hertzfeld-Doll. Maybe he was destined for the gossip-game after all. It may not have been intentional to implicate a successful woman in a male-dominated field, but another younger and even more passionate reporter was determined to call out Ames' gender bias and put to rest any shadow of impropriety cast upon Hertzfeld-Doll. If anyone deserved to be tainted it was Criss, surely his sly attempts at tax evasion were at best unpatriotic and at worst a symptom of his selfishly constructed materialistic lifestyle.

Rebecca Soundingham was still feeling the adrenaline course through her system as she tried to rehearse her introduction in her mind. Her legs were pumping under the small metal table, an old habit that would always present itself and give away her anxiety at the worst moments. Having easily swallowed half of her coffee already, she was jumpy.

Not that she needed the caffeine, Rebecca was already wound up. She was a sophomore at the University of Pennsylvania and even though she would answer "pre-law" when casually asked what she was majoring in, she believed herself to be a feminist rebel, an anarchist against the male dominated system. #FightingthePatriarchy was her go-to hashtag. She wanted justice, even though she had never personally been wronged, she felt the plight of every sister who was objectified, ridiculed, or treated to any other double-standard. Rebecca's wild curly hair fit the untamed thoughts in her mind.

Rebecca pulled out a small steno book from her back pocket and grabbed the pen that was laced through the metal spiral on top of the pack of paper. She clicked the pen to engage and quickly scribbled the date at the top of her pad of paper. "Monday, August 8th" She rose from her seat, too quickly, too suddenly, but she was already up and exposed. Her mind willed her body to stay on course, because this would be her only chance.

Rebecca wanted to be quiet, but not so quiet as to frighten her idol, sitting only ten yards from her. As she crossed over to the newest Justice, sitting idly in the almost empty cafeteria, Rebecca could feel her heart pounding. The best-case scenario would leave her with an exclusive interview and quickly debunk the celebrity gossip style of reporting that had created a national news frenzy over the weekend. In the worst case scenario, Capital police would imprison her for harassment of a sitting Justice.

She was only a few feet away. It was time to announce herself. Rebecca cleared her throat, but she did so too hard and now was coughing loudly. She reached out to balance herself on a chair, but her weight forced it to skid across the floor. A loud metallic scraping sound whined out from the chair as the metal grommets rubbed against the linoleum. Katherine turned to see what the commotion was. Concerned for the young woman quickly turning red in front of her, she stood up. Rebecca regained control of her breathing.

"Sorry, sorry to alarm you," she composed herself. "I am a sophomore at Penn, I'm studying to one day be a lawyer, like you." Rebecca had nailed the first sentence of her rehearsed speech, but Katherine was still standing. Rebecca couldn't tell if she was ready to run or not.

"My name is Rebecca Soundingham. I hate to bother you, but you are my idol," Rebecca immediately regretted this sentence as a wash of horror and fear appeared in Katherine's eyes. "I'm also a reporter. And I am disgusted by the story that Entertainment Weekly put out. That writer? Ames, he's rubbish." Rebecca could see her words of reassurance weren't helping to put Hertzfeld-Doll at ease.

"I wanted to tell the story from your side-" Katherine had cut Rebecca off with a quick wave of her hand.

"No comment," Katherine made her decision stern. "You may leave now."

"I'm not trespassing and I will leave you alone if that is your wish, but I know that the rumors flying around are all rubbish. If you would let me set the record straight this whole mess will be forgotten."

Katherine shook her head and pursed her lips. She began to pick up her lunch tray. Rebecca could see her chance slipping away. She grabbed for a folded piece of paper inside her jacket. Katherine saw her reach and began to panic. Rebecca slapped the old newspaper on the table. It was an old edition of the Daily Pennsylvanian, based on the headline article about students protesting, it was from Katherine's junior year at Penn. Katherine stopped for a moment to eye the document. "I found this in the newspaper archives on campus."

"I didn't write for the paper when I was a student, so we're not so alike." A small and polite smile finally crossed Katherine's face before quickly retreating. "I understand your ambition and I wish you luck in your academic and professional career, but I will not grant any interviews." Katherine was shorter than Rebecca had imagined. She was still in a fight-or-flight stance hunched over her cafeteria tray, protecting her sandwich. Rebecca was very aware that she could be seen as threatening or harassing, and she tried to make her point quickly. She had been forced into plan B very quickly into her introduction. This was not how she had planned the afternoon.

"I know you weren't a writer on the paper. I brought

that as a reference." Katherine was puzzled by Rebecca's elaboration. "It's the image that I thought would be of most interest to you. The image they selected was initially much larger, but since the main focus of the article was the protest, the extra bits were cut off." Katherine silently stared at Rebecca waiting for her to make her point.

Rebecca reached back into her jacket, Katherine visibly flinched and Rebecca realized her mistake again. She held out her left hand as a sign of peace as she reached into her pocket with the right. She held out the picture with her index finger and thumb holding up the far edge. "See the students on the far right of the frame?" Katherine leaned in, but was still out of striking distance.

"I've identified the young man in the brow line glasses as Jay Karkowitz and the handsome gentleman in front of him is Joseph Criss." Katherine nodded recognizing the names that Rebecca had read out. "And that woman walking next to Joseph, who appears to be laughing and smiling along with whatever the two men are laughing at," Rebecca paused hoping that she wouldn't have to finish the sentence, but she did. "That woman is you, Justice Hertzfeld-Doll. Although back then you were just Katie Doll."

She didn't need to spell it out for the woman, it was plain as day. The rumors indicated that Hertzfeld-Doll was not only a critical member of the founding of Criss Entertainment, but that her personal relationship with Joseph Criss was suspect. He was known as a playboy, even if they never had a romantic relationship, surely she must have been under his spell. Rebecca didn't believe any of it, but a second image of the two together would cause a resurgence of speculation. She felt dirty and grimy even making the implication, but she wanted her interview.

Katherine looked Rebecca square in the eyes. She raised an eyebrow as if daring her to try and publish the blurred edge of an outdated photo that proved nothing except that all three had in fact been enrolled at the University of Pennsylvania at the same time. "No comment." Katherine said firmly and walked away. Rebecca was intimidated. Katherine was a power, she had a force around her. Without having to say what was on her mind, the Justice was crystal clear. Rebecca nodded as she tried to fight back the urge to make numerous additional points as to why she should be granted an exclusive interview.

"But-" Rebecca stammered quickly, grasping at the last chance to maintain a conversation. "But, they are smearing you as a woman because you're smart and successful and he's handsome. That's it, that's all they have. You're letting them attack you as a woman-"

Hertzfeld-Doll whipped around quickly. The thin line of her frown pursed and she walked back to the young woman. Her steps were firm; her gait was measured. Rebecca forgot for a moment that the women approaching her was a guardian of justice and envisioned her as a cool and composed assassin with a deadly stare.

"Your flavor of feminism isn't the same as mine, young lady." Her words were short and to the point. No need to dally over rhetoric or intellectual postulates. Hertzfeld-Doll was shrewd and had no time for the nonsense reporting of a college student.

"You know; you have the power to make a statement that can change the shape of our fight. The media is making this about gender. *You're a woman, so you must have a romantic involvement, completely incapable of being impartial.* You have to respond. You can help thousands of women." Rebecca was proud of herself for taking the modern feminist stand, she was rallying the biggest ally for the cause. Regardless of her headline, Rebecca wanted to be the one to inspire that spark to action within the woman standing across from her. Her naïve and overly idealistic dreams were as easily whisked away as a bubble, just as fanciful and doomed to a short life.

Katherine looked at Rebecca directly. "This is off the record," she began in an even tone that was masking a deep well of frustration.

Rebecca's heart skipped a beat, her mind was racing to mentally record every last syllable that was about to be uttered.

"Because this is direct advice for you," she continued. "You have the power to change your own life and help yourself." The last words were spat out. Katherine turned and hurried away, irked by the intrusion. She would have to speak to security. She would have to speak to the alumni board. She would have to avoid all other people until this whole silly mess blew over.

Rebecca was startled and stunned by the attack in her

idol's words. She turned quickly and walked towards the exit. Embarrassed and exasperated, she wanted to fight back with words and display her impassioned belief that Hertzfeld-Doll was being unjustly portrayed in the media. Her notepad was haphazardly shoved into her pocket. She threw her coffee cup into the trash, not even noticing the recycling bin adjacent to it. Activists can only focus on one passion at a time. Rebecca was a sworn feminist; the environmentalists and recycle freaks could have her efforts in another decade.

<u>Thursday, December 31st, 1987</u>

Ron had been uncomfortable that whole evening. His tuxedo was dapper and sharp, but a large glob of toothpaste fell onto his lapel just minutes before they were supposed to leave for the party. Always punctual, Ron frantically changed into a black suit and found a tie that he would put on during the car ride over to the club. Katherine would drive so that she could help out with the effort. It should have been a clear omen for the evening.

The Hertzfelds departed only a few minutes behind their schedule. Ron and Katie were both very precise individuals and enjoyed keeping to a timeline. When the two arrived at the New Rochelle Country Club, fashionably late, and handed the keys to the valet, the night sky had become so dark that neither of them could see where the black sky and the shadowed trees parted. Ron was still flustered and said that his tie was too tight.

His awkward fidgeting pulled Katherine away from the calm splendor she saw in front of them. There were bright yellow lights and faint sounds of the jazz music coming from the banquet hall, wafting their way out onto the front steps to greet the couple. Katherine gave her husband a sweet smile and laid her hand on his arm. It was her usual method for helping him calm down. It only helped for a few moments, but it helped.

Katherine was at a loss for how to assist any further, but assumed a meal would put Ron's mind at rest. The menu for the evening was hors d'oeurves and cocktails. The fledgling company that Katherine sat on the board of was now flourishing, hence the New Year's Eve Gala. However, the board was wary of squandering too many of their profits on a three-course meal. The dancing and light refreshments would have to suffice for that year. The chairman of the board had notified all of the board members of this detail months ago, so Katherine was prepared to make her quick appearance and then duck out with Ron to enjoy a larger meal elsewhere.

She smiled at her husband and said, "T-minus one hour to a McDonald's drive-thru, honey." Ron smiled at her comment. His wife was all dressed up at a fancy event, in a gown that sparkled like the Adriatic in the moonlight, hair curled and pinned up, ears heavy with earrings that he had gifted her for Christmas, and now she was scheming to get a Big Mac as their last meal together for the year. The dichotomy wasn't lost on him and he chuckled. "Oh come on babe. It's New Year's Eve. We can spring for something a little nicer. How about Pizza Hut?"

"That's the spirit!" Katherine delighted, confident that she had appeased Ron for the moment. He had met some of the people in the room before. They were all the friends of Joseph Criss. The man had somehow converted his friends and acquaintances into co-founders and board members. It was almost as though he had been collecting them. A CPA, an actuary, a film-maker, and a writer. Ron spotted that Karkowitz fellow, he always seemed to be following Criss around like a puppy; happy to get the bedraggled scraps from the Alpha dog in the pack. Then, there was Katherine, the lawyer. Of all of the chairmen, Katherine was the only female among the co-founders. Ron was proud of her for being so fearless in the face of such a male dominated group. The fact that this was a male-dominated group wasn't lost on him either. And the fact that Joseph Criss was the leader of that group was certainly not a fact he would soon forget.

He saw how Katie was already facing an uphill battle in her day-to-day and having to fight for cases from less competent male contemporaries. Ron knew it wasn't as steep of an incline as it would have been a decade ago, and he wasn't a sissy male-feminist. But, he could still see the tenacity and potential in his wife and he would be damned if he let anyone keep her down. Ron knew that Katie was meant to shine, and fortunately, she would say the same of him. Their marriage was built on a bedrock of support. He still couldn't help but be protective of his wife, no matter how competent he knew her to be. The attitude of one, Joseph Criss, concerned him. He was a show-off, a braggart, and Ron didn't trust him in any matter. There was an undercurrent of worry fomenting within Ron, *would this man, Criss, cause a problem for Katherine?*

Ron started to loosen up his tie after he saw a few of the other gentlemen at the party, and he used the word generously. Most had shrugged off the idea of wearing a tux and opted to mimic Don Johnson with loose khakis, crew neck shirts, and overly casual blazers.

"The invitation did say black-tie optional, right?" Ron leaned in and whispered to his wife.

"It did," she said, wary herself of the long gown she had opted to wear. She saw that the younger girlfriends on the arms of the big-time investors were wearing mini-party dresses in loud prints that screamed for attention, or another hit of coke. Ron and Katie were too formal and once again the odd-ones out. They didn't like all of this flash and pizzazz. Not that the glitter wasn't exciting, but it was just that they had their own idea of what was truly golden. Katie smiled at Ron sheepishly, he read her mind.

"You look amazing," he calmed her insecurity and the feeling that she dressed too much like old lady, dressing out of her age group. Katie smiled and nodded her head toward her husband's. "What's the timer on the fast food?" Ron was hoping for a quick exit.

"It's only been 10 minutes," Katie said as they completed their first lap around the room.

Ron let out a deep sigh and then placed his hands on

his hips. "Well I'm off to find the champagne, it is New Year's Eve after all. I can count you in for a glass as well, my dear?" Ron had moved from his frustrated mood to his goofy, might-as-well-make-the-best-of-it mood. He made a flourish with his hand to mimic that of a waiter and he was off in search of some bubbly.

Katie stood quietly debating whether she should follow Ron or try to mingle and perhaps cut their wait time from 50 minutes down to 30 before leaving. She opted for the later. Katie shook hands with the wives of the more senior investors. She was glad that some of these women were much more polished and mature. And wearing gowns. Katie felt more in-step with them, they were her kind of people.

Within a few moments, she was spotted by the co-founders; a small circle of 3 men who had just stepped back inside from smoking cigars on the veranda. They reeked of heavy smoke and booze, but it was a party so she could forgive the apish drunken greeting. Jay and the two other co-founders, friends of Jay's from graduate school at USC, were in an uproar over whether one of them told a joke better than the other. Jay, of course, had added fuel to the fire by insisting that he was the originator of said joke. It was the usual antics for this group. Katie wondered how she had once found this repartee humorous when she was in college with Joseph and Jay.

Before the men could recite their comedic bit once more, Ron was back by her side with two flutes of champagne in hand. She quickly accepted and took a long sip. It was better to keep her mouth occupied so that she didn't have to continue to glue on her smile and reveal her indifference to what the men in front of her saw as hilarious.

Katie was unfortunately lumped in with this group often for meetings and photo-ops. Joseph insisted on naming her as a co-founder and then promptly installed her on the board of directors as well. "You're the one with the brains Dolly, I've got to keep you around so that I don't lose my business, or end up incarcerated," had been the reasoning provided and then it was never discussed again.

Jay and his cohorts soon found another couple to recite their act to. Katie was nervous about their behavior in front of investors. Most of them were the Manhattan young nouveau riche: they were loaded, financially and chemically. Only a few were Katie's type, serious business and legal professionals. These more established men had been charmed by Joseph's pitches, though they were very critical of the company's performance.

"I know you don't like it when I make these comments, but this feels more like a frat party than a corporate 'thank you for all the hard work this year'." Ron muttered as he stood aloof, one hand in his pocket, in the other was his empty champagne glass.

"For once, I'm not going to object. I think it's distasteful to put on a fancy event and then treat it like a regular ole weekend on the block." Katie had perfected her bored but frustrated look over many years of handling Joseph. That night she was resorting to her perfected slight smile and overly nice tone very quickly. Ron rubbed her bare arm and then gently laid his hand on the small of her back.

"Well, I'm here and you're here, so at least we're helping to class the place up." Ron made her laugh a bit. Katie smiled and kissed him sweetly on the cheek. They were having a moment, looking into each other's eyes as they were surrounded by twinkling lights. They were the calm statues in the middle of a hedonistic Greek forum with appalled on-lookers peering in from the fringe.

"We're almost halfway there," Katie said. "Although-"

"Welcome my gorgeous and generous guests!" Joseph Criss had entered from the far corner of the room and was making his grand speech. Katie would have to finish her thought after this interruption, although it was Joseph's party, so it was only an interruption to her and Ron.

-

That was how it had always been. Ever since those good ole college days. Katie was bookish and not very sociable. She had stumbled upon an acquaintance her freshman year with Joseph Criss. By virtue of her ability to resist and, at times, be repulsed by the charm that oozed from his pores, she was able to be around him without making a fool of herself. This made her one of very few females to actually make it into Joseph's circle of friends, although Katie didn't know about said circle until it was clear that she was in it. Being too inept at developing friendships, she figured she would stay.

Katie had loved her college years. The academic zeal and fervor that she felt all around her were ideal for her intellectual ambition. She would spend hours getting lost in the library, happy to be walking among the famous names and titles that she was eager to know more about. In her freshman year, she lived in the dorms as was required. Her roommate couldn't have been more anathema to Katie.

Anna was her name and she was peppy, and pretty, and athletic. She had perfected her crimped hair and spent an inordinate amount of time getting ready each day. Katie of course had her own plain neutral style. If she could have been compared to any pop-culture icon of the time, it would have to be Annie Hall. She didn't go for the ties or hats, but she did prefer neutral colors and was always in slacks. Katie was ready to take on the boys-club and dressed in defiance of common female norms.

It was on a quiet Sunday morning as Katie was engrossed inside a biography of James Madison that she heard a knock at the door. It was Anna, who had not only misplaced her room-key, but her wallet, and her school ID as well. Katie let Anna into the room, and promised to help her look for her missing items later in the afternoon. Anna insisted on taking a shower and napping first. This was just fine for Katie, because she had planned on spending a few more hours with the 4th President of the United States anyways. Anna quickly grabbed her towel and shower caddy and was gone. Katie assured her that she would keep the door unlocked so she could get back in without having to knock. *Now, back to Mr. Madison,* or so Katie thought.

About ten minutes later, there was another knock at the door. Katie rolled her eyes figuring that Anna had forgotten that the door had been left unlocked. Katie dog-eared the book page, sprang up to her feet, and opened the door. The counterpart to her perky, pretty roommate stood before her. He was tall with dark features, handsome as all hell, with curly brown hair, and dressed very well for a college-man. Katie felt very unprepared and underdressed, just wearing her pajama shorts and t-shirt. "Can I help you?" she managed a polite and domestic tone.

"Yeah, I'm looking for Anna, I'm sorry if I have the wrong room."

"Oh no, this is her room. I'm her roommate, Katie. She's in the shower. You can come back later or leave a message."

"Phew," the man sighed and made his way into the room without being invited. "Good, I found her stuff in the common room of my floor. I figured I would return it, but I don't want to see her. She was hard-core flirting with my roommate last night, clingy type of girl. Shame because she's pretty, she'd be better off trying the hard-to-get approach. I just don't want to field any questions from her." He leaned against the desk chair as he gave his thorough synopsis of Anna's mating techniques.

"Well, I'll let her know that an R.A found her items and returned them, that way she won't think that-" Katie trailed off her sentence hoping for the strange man to introduce himself.

He eyed her up like a construction man ogling a passing woman. Katie wasn't offended though; something told her that he was doing an overall survey more than taking a piggish eye-full. "Oh sorry-," he said as though snapping out of a trance. "Joseph Criss." He extended his hand for a handshake.

"Katherine Doll. Most people call me Katie." They shook hands.

"Eh, I'm gonna call you Dolly. You look like a porcelain doll, you know that? You should try playing that up for a costume party one time."

"Thanks Joe-" Katie began.

"Joseph." He corrected.

"Thanks Joseph, I'll keep that in mind. And as I mentioned, I'll tell a little white lie to keep both you and *your* roommate safe from *my* roommate, for now." Katie's short span of patience had been spent.

"Thanks Dolly. Well I don't want to be here when Anna gets back," He said striding back to the door as though he owned the place and could come and go as he pleased. "See ya around Dolly," he said with a wink as he left.

Katie sat back on her bed somewhat mystified and

bewildered. He was obviously one of those overly confident and therefore flawed men that seemed to always stumble into success. Katie had resisted men like that her whole life because, while they were very aesthetically appealing, their personalities were often repulsive. But, Joseph Criss wasn't so bad. Katie caught herself admiring his candor and ease of conversation. Right as she began to form and spell out her first impression of him in her mind, Anna walked back into the room. She was mildly dried off, but for the most part still sopping wet in her thick robe with her hair up in a towel.

"Feel better?" Katie asked. Anna was clearly suffering from a mild hangover. Katie handed Anna a bottle of water from the mini-refrigerator and an aspirin.

"Hmm, kinda. I'm worried about my room key and ID. I don't want to have to pay for a new one."

"Oh, someone dropped them off while you were in the shower."

Anna quickly looked over at them sitting on her bed. "Joe?!" she asked with a twinkle in her eye and her face lit up. Joseph, Katie corrected her roommate in her mind. *Mr. Criss must have told a little white lie himself*, she thought.

"It could have been I guess. It was an R.A. I didn't get his name."

"Oh," she sighed. "How did you know it was an R.A. if he didn't say his name?" Anna was a full-on detective when it came to investigating every move and subtle action of a male that she had her sights on. Katie had seen her do this once or twice before in the first two months of college. Even though she had some annoying habits, she was nice and mildly entertaining. Anna was most entertaining when dissecting the motives of a man.

"He had a Res. Life shirt on," Katie answered as though lying was as natural as the truth. A quality she had possessed for quite some time. She had only ever used it for good though, it was very helpful when planning her mother's surprise 50th birthday party. It would also come in handy in many legal negotiations years later.

"Hmm," Anna said mulling over this piece of evidence in her head. "What Res. Hall did he work in?"

"I don't know. He didn't say," Katie shrugged her shoulders as she began to place her schoolbooks in her shoulder bag.

"Okay. I may question you more later, but for now I need to sleep."

"Well, I'll be at the library for a few hours, so that should give you some time," Katie smiled as she began to brush out her ridiculously long and always frizzy blonde hair. "So who was the prince charming you were hoping had stopped by?"

Anna hesitated for a moment. Truthfully, Katie hadn't been a good roommate in terms of girl talk. Although, she knew that sometimes a good roommate is one who is somewhat removed, but still pleasant. Anna decided to let Katie in and told her all about her latest crush.

"Joseph Criss! Oh gosh, he is so gorgeous. He's from some middle of nowhere town, but I heard he's got an uncle, or a family friend, or something-or-other in

Hollywood, and when he graduates he's already got a job lined up out there working for some major production company. He's so dreamy Katie. His roommate is cute too, can you imagine the luck? If we ever go out, we can do a double date." She went on for a bit telling Katie about how she met him in the dining hall, and how he was so cute, and that his roommate invited her to a party on their floor.

"So of course, I had to go and I spent most of the night talking to him and he was into everything I was saying. He's such a good listener. I bet we'll tell our kids about how we met at college. I think I could handle the Hollywood lifestyle. But, oh gosh, the best thing. So of course I was more than a little drunk last night. And I was probably being a little pushy with trying for a kiss or even more. But he wouldn't kiss me. And when I started to get the spins, he put me to sleep in his bed and he and his roommate slept out in the common room. How gentlemanly." She actually swooned after this and fell back onto her bed.

"Sounds like a fairytale if I ever heard one," Katie actually managed to sound sincere. She walked out of their small room and left Anna to her daydreams and real dreams about the handsome Mr. Joseph Criss. Although Katie did have to wonder, after his open evaluation of how Anna had behaved, why did he say that she was after his roommate and not him? Katie pondered this unnecessary farce for a moment as she walked to the library in the last warm afternoon of the fall. Once she had arrived at her favorite cubicle and unloaded her notebooks, she pushed Mr. Criss and all of his curiously constructed words out of her mind.

Years later, as Katie stood waiting for Joseph to finish his speech at the New Year's Eve gala, she would try to not zone-out. But that was difficult to do. His toast had run on too long.

-

At last, Joseph Criss concluded, raised his glass, everyone took a sip, and the evening resumed as though someone had clicked the button on their VCR. Ron was gently rubbing on Katie's arm and was hoping to softly persuade her to leave. Their moment was interrupted by a jovial shout, "Ah, my guests of honor! The Hertzfelds!"

Ron and Katie looked over to see a smiling Joseph Criss coming their way, channeling the flair and style of Jay Gatsby, with his arms spread wide. He draped his arm over Ron's shoulder and with the gracefulness of a typhoon took over their conversation.

"I'm so glad that you both could make it. It wouldn't be the same without you here. You know Ron, it was our Dolly who made this all happen. Without her, I would have gone under from astronomical fees and back taxes."

Ron smiled and said, "Don't you have accountants to handle the taxes?"

Joseph batted down his words with his free hand, "You know what I mean, right Dolly?" This was the moment when Ron and Katie were separated momentarily by the large personality of Joseph Criss that a photo was taken of the CEO and one of his board members. The photo would run in the society pages the following day. Many, many years later that same photo would be used to pit Joseph against Katie and implicate them both in a nonsense scandal with no merit or substance.

"Exactly." Katie smiled to pacify the situation, she was still trying to blink away the large patches that filled her eyes after the flash of the camera. Standing there was overconfident, and overbearing, Joseph Criss trying to coax some friendly tidings out of her darling husband. "Thank you for inviting us to this party. It gave us a chance to wear our best for the evening, although we are both terribly hungry, we may duck out early," she tried to sound disappointed, but Ron saw through her thin veil of politeness.

"Oh no! You gotta stay! Ron, tell her you've gotta stay! We're gonna have a great view of the fireworks! Right out there on the deck," Joseph was pointing, his arm almost covering Ron's face.

"Oh, I wouldn't worry about that," Ron said as he moved Joseph's arm away. "I know I'm gonna have the best view in town." He was staring at Katie, deeply, unflinching, unmoving. The heat in his eyes causing his wife to blush. She smiled at him as if to say, "oh stop it, you flatter me too much." She reached out for Ron's hand.

"Well, hopefully you can stay. It would be great to

celebrate with everyone." Joseph was either completely oblivious, or he was taking the hint to extricate himself quickly. "Speaking of which, I need to make some more rounds. Be sure to say goodbye before you leave." Joseph was gone just as quickly as he had crashed their private party. Katie didn't take her eyes off of Ron, so she wasn't sure where anyone else in the room was at the moment. Within a few moments the Hetzfelds had finished their champagne, found their coats, and given their ticket to the valet for their car.

-

Katie ran into Pizza Hut to pick up a hot pie with extra cheese and sausage while Ron kept the car running and warm. They ate their pizza in their fancy attire on the carpet of their living room in front of a lit fire. They watched as their television displayed images of fireworks shown across the world. It was 1988 at last! After eating a few slices, they recounted their favorite moments of the evening. The two giggled as they exchanged impressions of the intoxicated people at the Criss Entertainment Holdings party and the look that the teenager at Pizza Hut gave Katie as she glided into the restaurant dressed to the nines. They discussed their resolutions and toasted to another year together. The couple killed a bottle of merlot and made their way upstairs for a final celebration of their own.

In the quiet that followed, as they lay on their bed,

and welcomed the cool air that always seemed to leak in through the windows, Katie wrapped her arms around her husband. Content, smiling, and without any worries, the couple lay wrapped up in the silent wonder of their evening together. Ron gently stroking the golden hairs above Katie's temple, Katie lightly scratching Ron's forearm. They soothed each other and surrounded each other.

"So, overall, I would say this was a successful evening," Katie said with a smile.

"I would say everything after the party was a success, actually." Ron added.

"Very true, you can't beat a romantic dinner for two." Katie paused to distinguish her playful remarks from her more serious ones. "I'm sorry the party was more trouble than it was worth. At least I got to wear my fancy dress!" Katie smiled as she thought back on her floor length gown. She would need to have it dry cleaned if she let it get wrinkled.

"That dress was good, but it only looked great once you put it on!" Ron said with a gentle squeeze around her waist. "I don't know, the party was nice, but it was the people. Just not my style, honey."

"Not mine either, but it's part of the business I guess. I wouldn't mind being able to step away from it all."

"You know, you have the ability to do that." Ron reminded Katie.

"Hmm, maybe I will then." Katie said in a non-comital tone.

"No Dolly no! Don't go Dolly!" Ron began to tickle Katie as he put on his best attempt to impersonate Joseph's dry voice. He wasn't too far off the mark. Katie giggled and bounced and moved with each tickle. Ron loved the way she moved when she laughed. Once this small match ended, Katie was exasperated and Ron was smiling proudly.

"I take it you don't like that nickname?" Katie asked with a half-laugh, still recovering.

"No, I've never really cared for it." Ron said in a matter of fact tone. Katie understood what he meant right away. It wasn't that he didn't care for the nickname, she knew that he didn't care for Joseph. It had been a fact Katie was hoping to delay realizing for a while, but it was now clear that it was more than just a general dislike. It was an actual and true feeling that wouldn't go away over time and acquaintance. Ron would never like Joseph and he would certainly never like the way he spoke to Katie. In that moment he said it all, Ron made it clear that he didn't like any affiliation between his wife and Joseph Criss. The ties were severed. Katherine didn't even need to consciously make a decision. She didn't need to sigh and say "Okay if that's what you want". It was a silent agreement that didn't need any thought or discussion. Katie leaned over and kissed her husband. There was no line that Ron could draw that Katie would question. This was the only one that he had yet to draw, and it was a clearly defined border.

"Well then, you'll have to make sure to give me a

better one then."

"I already have the best name to call you babe, and that's Mrs. Hertzfeld." Katie lit up with a smile and the two fell asleep holding each other. Eventually Katie rolled over onto her side and fidgeted with her pillows. Ron moved slightly and pushed some of the sheets off of him when he began to feel warm. But throughout the night they stayed connected, just as they were always connected.

After all that time, it was never a lattice-work of intricately woven emotions in a love triangle. It was always a clear line connecting Katie and Ron; it was infinite and constantly gaining energy as the years passed.

Joseph was the outsider looking in because there was no love there. He didn't love Katherine or pine for her, he didn't even particularly lust for her. All that he wanted was to prove that he could make her second guess; make her blink and question. That was always his game. The reason that he would insinuate a connection between them with college friends, the reason he would call her late at night. It was his game to play with his Dolly and see if he could get a reaction. But that never happened. Katie never once felt tempted or drawn to Joseph in any way and so, silently and without an explanation to Joseph, without even debating that he needed an explanation, Katherine put up a wall that was brick and expansive. She looked only to Ron and never looked back until a smart reporter tried to dig everything up.

<u>Monday</u>

It was late in the evening. Even though she had a book in her hand and her eyes were looking at the words, her mind was elsewhere. Her workday had ended silently. She did receive some consoling advice from another Justice, whose name does not need to be pulled through the mud. However, having another female to speak to, even if they were on opposite sides of the political spectrum, made Katherine feel slightly better. Sitting in one of the easy chairs of Katherine's office, she was reminded that Clarence Thomas sat on the Court for decades after the Anita Hill scandal, which was an actual scandal. The current news was making a mountain out of a molehill with the Criss case. Katherine smiled for the first time in days and thanked her colleague for her encouraging words. She wondered out loud if any of this would have come up if she had helped a female classmate start a business. "You can bet it wouldn't," she was reminded. "That story line wouldn't be nearly as entertaining for the media roaches to feast on."

She let her mind wander from feminist rhetoric to her memories of how this had unfolded. Nothing had seemed like a mistake along the way. She had broken no laws. On their first meeting, Joseph had named her "Dolly", a play on her last name and he often bellowed at her from across campus, down hallways, and at times in the library: "Hellooooo Dolly!" as though he was the best Louis Armstrong impersonator to ever live. She never bestowed a nick-name upon him and always called him Joseph. Everyone always called him Joseph.

By their sophomore year she had the unpleasant task of tutoring Joseph in basic microeconomics. His inability to sit still and his constant diversions, what might today be labeled as ADHD, made him a frustrating pupil. Katie did her best. She certainly never backed down from a challenge. Although, she might have preferred to have never been asked to take that one on at all.

Her few female friends, her fellow classmates, and at times complete strangers would approach her and ask to be introduced to Joseph. She never understood how women would fawn over him. Though he was by the book what Hollywood kept saying was attractive, she found him to be lacking something. She puzzled over this, wondering if perhaps she was missing the gene that told her to go weak in the knees for a square jaw and a winning smile. His inability to focus, the value that he placed on relationships over knowledge, and his insistence on finding a new diversion were personality traits that she would never be able to relate to. But, she let those errant thoughts leave her brain as she kept focused on her goals and her studies.

It wasn't until a friend, one of her closest, and someone she thought of as level headed, began to obsess over Joseph that she finally gave into one request and made an attempt to set them up. It was a disastrous endeavor from the onset. But what evolved from this was the beginning of the beguiling game. There would often be a lingering stare of confusion from Joseph, a question in his eyebrows that wouldn't cross his lips. At first Katie was confused, and almost let herself believe the rouse that was being constructed.

It took Katie some time to figure out the motive behind Joseph's deceptions. This illusion was a costly one, as it would ultimately force an impasse and end their personal and professional relationship. It was this ugly disguised game that Joseph started that was the cause of all of the chaos currently impacting them both so acutely.

Katherine was pondering the past quietly when she heard the car pull into the driveway. She had pulled back her hair into a loose bun and had kicked off her heels, but she was still wearing the same blouse and slacks that she had worn to work. She made a point to finish the paragraph that she was reading and mark it, so that she could find her place later. Just as she was closing the book in her hand around the small slip of paper she was using as a bookmark, Ron sauntered in through the side entrance from the garage.

"Well honey, I may stink like a fish, but today I feel like a man!" Ron puffed out his chest and let a big bear of a smile spread across his face.

"Oh yeah? Did all of the other hominids back at the cave bow down to your superior skills?" Katie responded playfully as she stood up from their rich and deeply cushioned couch. She strode easily into the kitchen and gently embraced her husband, who very quickly wrapped one arm around her and dipped her.

"Yeah baby, I'm the King of the tribe!" He laid a big wet kiss on her lips before swinging her back onto her feet.

"Well King fisher, best hunter of all men, you do stink. But I love you anyways!"

Ron guffawed. "Well I guess I'd better go and clean up for my Queen." She smiled and watched him head out of the kitchen and make his way up the stairs; she heard them creak and snap with each heavy step.

Katherine waited a few minutes before she followed. She began to undress in the bedroom and put away her jewelry from the day before slipping into a discreet sleeping gown. Women her age called them sleeping gowns, they weren't flannel granny pajamas, nor were they nighties. A woman her age had to be realistic, gravity had begun to take effect on her once perfectly perky breasts and plump behind. She had her full length satin sleeping gowns, slinky but modest. She sauntered into the bathroom and sat on the closed toilet while Ron was in the shower and began to ask him about his day.

"Eh, George called around noon to go out to the lake, so that took up most of the day. I got some writing in this morning though, which felt," he paused as if searching for the correct word, "refreshing."

"Yeah?"

"Yeah," answered Ron's voice from behind the opaque shower curtain. "I was beginning to worry that my block wouldn't lift, but it did."

"That's great to hear honey. I can't wait to read your

next chapter once it's done."

The water stopped and Katherine could hear the lingering droplets dripping off of every surface in the shower. The curtain swiped open. Katie looked up at her husband and smiled, handing him the towel that had been folded neatly on the toilet seat before she sat down.

"Thank you!" Ron smiled back. While some couples grow old and cynical as the years pass, the Herztfelds only grew sweeter.

"No problem," Katie replied easily. She started to get up to give Ron some space to dry off.

"And thank you for helping this morning." His tone was less easy.

"What?" Katie asked quickly.

"My writer's block." Ron's face said it all; he was debating saying the next sentence out loud. Katie had already spotted this so he decided to say it, and not cause additional questions.

"All of this business with that Criss... asshole." Finally, he said how he had always felt about him out loud. It only took three decades "And this insinuation that you two are somehow still friends or whatever-"

"You know that-" she began to defend herself.

"I know." Ron's answer was definitive and his eyes were beginning to change, the mood still revealing itself to Katie.

"You've earned so much on your own. I know you say that you couldn't have done as much without me. But you earned this Katie. I hate to see that man-child put that in jeopardy. I know I never said it out loud, but your ability to sever all ties with him so swiftly made it clear to me a long time ago that you were a serious woman. You knew what you wanted, and I was humbled, and still am, that what you wanted was me. So, as I was processing this over breakfast, you inspired me. You, and all that you have done, and what you did all those years ago. Heck, we could have been millionaires by now if you had stayed on and kept your shares, but you cut him out cold. I should be the best man for you and your greatness. So my inspiration was amplified by you."

She walked directly over to him and kissed him. Her arms wrapping around him slid down his back, still wet from the shower.

"You never had to ask. I knew it was no choice at all. You're my husband." She hated that Ron ever doubted, that he thought there could have been room in her heart for another. She wanted him to see within her mind. She wanted him to understand that any jealousy was never warranted. But she had to use her words, and decades earlier she had used her actions. It wasn't until that night she realized that it had worked, that she had shown Ron exactly what she needed to: no other would ever tempt her love away from him.

-

At about the same time, Justin Ames was getting laid into by his editor on the West Coast. The article had been breaking news on Friday afternoon and had fueled all of the weekend news programs. ET, Extra, and Meet the Press all had multiple segments dedicated to the details that he had exposed. But, Monday brought radio silence as no new details emerged. An online petition had been started to force Katherine Hertzfeld-Doll to recuse herself from the case, but only 150 people had signed it by 2pm.

It was at that time that Ames was called into his editor's office. Bruce Unger was a capable man, he was into obscure music, and had his ideals hardened after years of seeing the grimy real world of Hollywood. Now, as he stood behind his desk, he was red in the face. "Do you know who I just got off the phone with?"

Before Ames could respond with a wise-aleck answer, he heard the answer in a loud resonating yell. Justin immediately wished that the editor's office wasn't made entirely of glass, because now everyone else was going to see the verbal lashing that was in store for him.

"Jay Karkowitz, JAY KARKOWITZ! He just got off the phone with me explaining that his lawyer, who also happens to represent Joseph Criss and Criss Entertainment will be on his way over this afternoon to discuss the definition of *libel*."

Ames sat silently for a moment, wanting to be sure that his editor wasn't about to start in on the next part of his rant. "All of the facts were confirmed, I didn't publish a single libelous item. I laid out the facts and asked the questions. I didn't draw any connections that weren't supported. If others are making those connections, then they can answer for it."

"This man owns Hollywood!" The editor pounded his hand on the desk and Ames saw the files shake with the reverberations. They began to slide sloppily across his desk from their disheveled piles. There was a vein at the top of Unger's forehead that was beginning to plump up as he continued to shout. Justin Ames wanted to say the obvious, you approved the story, but he bit his lip.

"The way I see it, they don't like that I exposed something they were hoping to keep quiet. The truth can be inconvenient that way. If Jay and his lawyer are headed this way, then maybe they would like to be interviewed to set the record straight."

Ames was unwavering. Unger took a deep breath and the vein in his forehead began to recede behind his deep-set wrinkles. "This was a great story, and I agree they are nervous. But this isn't the Wall Street Journal or the New York Times. We aren't equipped for a legal battle with Criss, Karkowitz, or the Supreme Court of the United States!"

Ames sat quietly. His jaw was set and he was clenching his teeth. "So, what would you like me to do?"

"Finish out this story, you'll cover the entire trial until it ends. At which point I will accept your resignation and write you a favorable recommendation for any other publication you want." Unger sighed as the words came out of his mouth.

"Are you kidding me?" Ames about jumped out of his

chair. "I brought in over five million hits to our website in under 3 days with that story. We have news shows promoting the magazine by mentioning it over and over. It's free publicity and it's a damned good story. And you want me out?" Ames was loud, louder than he should have been. He could feel the eyes of everyone in the office on the back of his head and this debate, now an all-out fight, was being played out for everyone to see.

"Criss Entertainment pays for 50% of our advertising budget." His editor's words were cool and direct. He looked at Ames with the wisdom of a haggard man, who had seen the ways of the world and was trying to explain it to someone who might be able to navigate the terrain without becoming jaded.

Ames stood up and stared directly at his boss. It took him a full 30 seconds of standing still to muster the courage to take his next action.

"I quit." Ames turned around and started toward the door. No handshake, no 'thank you for the opportunity'. Ames had his hand on the door, ready to pull it open by the handle and turned.

"Sellout," he muttered and he walked directly to his desk. Grabbed his few personal items, his folder on the Criss/Hertzfeld-Doll connection, and walked out. He didn't wave good-bye to any coworkers, he didn't flip anyone off as he rushed to the elevator. He simply left, and with him he took his journalistic ambition and the offer for the favorable recommendation.

<u>Tuesday</u>

Katie didn't sleep very well. She hadn't been sleeping well for the past few nights. She knew in her mind that she could be impartial in this case, and she had already discussed her decision to stay on the case with the Chief. She wouldn't let public opinion sway her, much as her predecessors had never let outside influences interfere with the Court. A bastion of liberty and justice, she had a greater standard to uphold for the American people, and she had centuries of honored justices to serve as her inspiration.

She kept telling herself that after a quiet Monday, that the story was about to blow over. No one would remember this in a week. Still, her sleep was tenuous and she only dreamt briefly. Her dream wasn't really a dream even, but a memory. Of the day that defined her ability to be impartial in this case, the day that she severed her ties with Criss Entertainment Holdings, stock symbol CEH on the S&P 500.

She had taken her lunch break to venture out of the office and head further uptown to the New York offices of Criss Entertainment. She had been there almost monthly for board meetings and this would be her final visit. Even if she wasn't signing away her stake in the company, she wouldn't be able to pop over to the office anymore. The entire operation was moving from New York to Los Angeles. When she arrived at the 8th floor, she saw the usually bustling office moving at a much slower pace. Desks were packed up and several staff members were taking time to stop and chat together.

Katie waved at those she recognized and headed straight for the desk of Melissa Ortiz. Impossibly bright and bubbly all the time, Melissa greeted Katie with a warm smile and showed her directly into Joseph's office.

"Oh no, I'm just here to sign some paperwork today. I don't have a meeting set up with Mr. Criss." Katie corrected Melissa.

"He told me that he wanted to meet with you first. You know he's been terrorizing HR all week. He won't let any of the applicants for Chief Counsel past the first stage of screening. He's been tearing up all of their resumes." After Katie had told Joseph that she couldn't stay on the board, he told her that he was just about to offer her the position as top lawyer for the company. He wanted her to stay on full-time, not just in an advisory manner. She persisted that she couldn't deviate from her career path, based on Melissa's insights, Joseph was not going to be easily swayed.

"Well, I would be flattered if it were coming from any other person. You know how Joseph gets when he tries to make a point," Katie gave Melissa a knowing nod.

Melissa rolled her eyes and gave a smile back. An unspoken agreement between the two that, yes, Joseph could be a bit theatrical. She directed Katie into Joseph's massive corner office and asked if she would like any water or coffee. Katie declined as she had been planning to be in and out of the office within fifteen minutes. It seemed that wouldn't be the case anymore.

Katie tried to keep her thoughts calm, but she was angry. Angry with Joseph for this last minute change; and angry with him for nine years of his game. In this one-sided game, Katie's nickname appeared to become more and more apt with time. In college, Dolly was what Joseph called her, and this was when the game had begun. She would hear from classmates that she and Joseph were somehow involved, which was a work of fiction. When she responded, "oh of course not, just ask Joseph," she would be shocked to hear their response, "who do you think told us?" There was his abject rejection and often hatred of any man that she would date, which seemed over the top once she began to examine what was being constructed around her.

The person who had grown into a friend, had made good on his promise. He would go off and play with the loose coeds and have his follies and antics. And when he was bored he would pick up and play with his Dolly. He would hope to hook her on his line with no intention of ever reeling her in. He would play with her as though she was a source of amusement.

It took Katie until her second year of Law School to realize this pattern. Katie was beginning to grow tired of dismissing the odd comments and hugs that came out of nowhere and lasted too long. She didn't like having to answer questions about her friendship with Joseph because it never made sense to the pretty darlings who wanted those hugs so desperately.

Then Joseph decided to take his game to the next level. While he was living out in New York City he would frequently call Katie. The drunk midnight calls that would result in serenades of the latest hits; Tom Petty was his favorite. With the birth of the answering machine Katie would find herself playing back a 20-minute one-sided conversation from Joseph at least once a month. She had learned to laugh, but always felt that slight pull, that question of, "what is all of this for?" Katie would allow herself only a few minutes to try and piece together the puzzle that Joseph Criss was becoming, and then she would force herself to concentrate on her class-work.

Katie made plans to move to New York after graduation from Law School and Joseph was excited to help her move, even signing up to offer his assistance before she had even found an apartment in the city. She would graduate, spend a month studying for the bar exam, and once she passed, she would be off to France for three weeks. Her life was running along as planned.

Not even a year later, Dolly had agreed to help when Joseph decided to go into business for himself. Joseph spent several weeks requesting her legal help with the initial paperwork for incorporation. The whole gang was chipping in. Jay was going to head up operations. Joseph had a plan. And that plan inevitably led to Katie and Ron, her handsome husband, to the New Year's Eve party. This led to the plain statement from Ron that he had never liked the nickname 'Dolly' that Joseph had bestowed upon her. Seeing the full view of what it meant now, Katie could understand why he didn't like it. She was starting to resent it as well.

After a few minutes of these thoughts, Katie heard a knock on the door from behind her. Joseph was standing at the entrance to his office. Tall and cool, the light coming in from the windows was shining on his face. He looked much the same as that first morning when they had met by accident many years earlier. He eyed her up and down again, the same way he had taken her in initially.

"Hey Dolly," his words were low and exhausted. He smiled in a peculiar way, the strange smile that often accompanied Joseph's attempts to manipulate Katie. "I'm sad that you're here. I'm sad that once this meeting ends you'll no longer be a part of our company."

Katie tried so hard to not roll her eyes and let the disdain building within her boil over. She had waited for too long to say anything, and now she needed a clean cut. No nasty arguments or accusations. Just a clear end to this game, and a final declaration that he could hold no sway over her.

"Joseph, you know how busy I am. I don't take my commitments lightly. It's not fair to you and the team if I can't keep up my end of the bargain." Katie took a deep breath and applauded mentally for her display of cool and finesse.

Joseph finally entered the office, but instead of going to sit behind his desk, as a professional would, he sat in the chair next to Katie and leaned in towards her. "I was planning to come in here and offer anything and everything to get you to stay with the company."

At this, he reached for her hands, which were folded in her lap. She moved them away quickly, it was almost a precognitive motion. The smooth contours of Joseph's face hardened. In all of the years that she had never considered him, this was the first direct rejection she had ever dealt him. The muscles just above his jaw were twitching. She could sense that he was angry. A child who suddenly realizes that he had worn out the batteries on his favorite toy usually tries to coerce it by slamming it on the ground, correct?

Katie could feel his frustration, the tension between them was thick. She was happy to be establishing a clear boundary, finally. It was incessantly uncomfortable in that office.

"I can see your mind has been made up," he stood and moved over to the cabinet behind his desk quickly. "But who has made it for you, I can only guess." Joseph thumbed through the files that lay on top of the cabinet and selected one thin folder. The accusation in his words was enough to set Katie off.

"What do you mean by that?" She was sharp, dissecting his words.

"You know exactly what I mean," his entire tone had shifted. Usually so juvenile and playful around her. It was clear that Mr. Criss, the businessman, had showed up to the meeting. She had only very rarely seen him behave in this direct manner.

She opened her mouth to speak, but nothing came

out. She remembered that the door to the office was open and that she would need to watch her next words very carefully, so as not to spark a screaming-match. She knew what he meant: Ron.

Joseph was implying that Ron was forcing her to cut her ties to the company. Which was a half-truth. Ron's distrust of Joseph had been the final straw. But, Katie had never fully trusted Joseph, and Ron was worried that being connected to him in business would one day be costly for her. Katie looked down at her hands, bound tightly in her lap, with the tension of a vice grip, they were still and steady. She was never good with confrontation, she expected to be shaking.

Joseph must have read the silence on her part as an admission of guilt. In reality, it was Katie taking the time to calculate her next move. Joseph pounced at his perceived opportunity. He was standing behind the desk, his weight forward and he leaned on the surface with his fists. He stood up straight and walked back around to the other side of the table with the thin file in hand.

"Katie," he said her actual name for the first time in their entire warped friendship. He handed her the file and crouched down in front of her. "I'll call you Katie, I'll call you Katherine," he started to ooze charm. It was as though he could control the release of his own hormones and amino acids to draw from his stores of manipulation on cue. "I wanted to build this company with you, and it was a desperate attempt to keep you at best, but I had to keep you Katie. You've always been my Katie."

She had kept her eyes locked on her hands until this moment. In an instant she looked into his eyes and saw the same smoky-green that had persuaded her so many times before. Lie to your roommate for me. *Help me study again. Promise me you'll write. File the incorporate papers for me.* All part of his calculated persuasion. His tone was dead-on, his words were perfect. Almost as though they had come out of some sappy soap opera. Sure, it would make the girls swoon, but Katie was a woman, and a lawyer, and knew when she was being fooled with. This was a skill that would serve her well in her career as a Judge.

When their eyes met, she could see Joseph visibly relax, as though that was the secret key to her continued servitude. In his mind he was almost home-free, and on his way to keeping his decade-long game running. She opened the file in her hands, knowing full-well that with the swift motion of a pen she would be able to leave. Joseph was distracted, building the finale of his performance.

He smiled softly, again a performance worthy of a Daytime Emmy. Katie smiled too, but for a very different reason. This final scene, his blatant toying with her mind to try to prove that he could control her, it was sickening. She was the only one to blame for allowing it to go on for so long. She smiled because she was going to be free very soon.

As Joseph reached his right hand up, reaching for her temple to touch her hair, Katie quickly grabbed a pen from the end of his desk, twisted it open and signed the first page. She flipped quickly to the next tabbed page and began to sign. Joseph stopped mid-reach.

"What are you doing Dolly?" She could have been burning the Bible given his tone and shock. She continued to sign and date two more times without answering him. "What?-" He never finished that final question.

She closed the file and stood up quickly, gracefully. She looked down on him, still low to the ground. His jaw was open as he synthesized a shocked and betrayed expression.

She placed the pen back on the desk and at the same time said, "I'm not your Dolly anymore." It was a truth that was as easy to say as a lie. She was firm and her words were final.

Katie turned and left. There was no pause for effect, no dramatic music playing behind her. When she thought back on that moment she often pictured herself adding a flare to her motion to emphasize her words, but they needed no decoration. She walked over to Ms. Ortiz and handed her the file with the signed paperwork. She smiled and wished her well in Los Angeles. She headed to the elevator and kept her eyes forward. She didn't want to see if Joseph was staring at her longingly from his office. She didn't want to see if he was running after her. She didn't want to see if he was anywhere in sight.

She was free from his manipulation from that moment forward.

Katherine woke with an uneasy calm. She was confident and composed and knew that no matter how this momentary frustration might cause her stress now, that she would change none of her actions if given the chance.

She prepared for the day, dressed slowly, and set her hair before she joined her husband in the kitchen. He was busy cooking breakfast. They both usually opted for a healthy meal on weekdays with an extravagant brunch on weekends, but she could smell the savory aroma of bacon that Tuesday morning.

"Mmm, smells delicious Ron!" A smile broke across her face as she peered over his shoulder to inspect the sizzling strips of fat.

"Well you deserve a delicious breakfast. And I like bacon." Ron gestured for her to sit down. Two tall glasses of orange juice were set on their ottoman, the morning newspaper folded in between them. The television was on with the morning cable news playing.

"Ugh, can I change the channel?" Katie was dreading another morning filled with speculative and frustrating reports over her "involvement" in "business dealings" with Joseph Criss.

"Hmm, I don't think so." Ron called from the kitchen.

"Right, I have to face the day and know what they're saying to be better prepared when college kids accost me for an interview." This was a statement but it was spoken as a question to her husband.

"Nope," Ron walked into the living room with full plates in is hand.

"Why then?" Katie felt exhausted at the idea of enduring additional scrutiny in front of her husband.

"Because," he sat down and positioned the plates by the glasses of orange juice. "Everyone deserves a bit of good news now and again." He handed her the newspaper. It had been opened to the current events section. A thin article to the left side of the front page filled in the rest for Katie.

A public relations statement from Criss Entertainment Holdings.

From the desk of Joseph Criss:

I am appalled by the recent accusations regarding the involvement of a certain dedicated public servant with a sterling reputation. All business development efforts in the creation and founding of Criss Entertainment Holdings were professional and business like. As I said in my letter to the shareholders when one of our original co-founders elected to step down in order to pursue their career at full-speed, we respectfully parted ways and the remaining co-founders gave their full support to Katherine.

With that thin article the story seemed to evaporate quickly. Some of her clerks took to calling her "sterling" for a few days. "Here are your sterling briefs Justice." "How was your sterling lunch?" She smiled at their humor and was glad to be laughing with them and not the butt of their joke. The news channels found something new to focus on and soon Katherine was able to focus on the upcoming Judicial season.

About a week or so later, she was contacted about a blog article that had sprung up with a crazy conspiracy theory about a romantic involvement between Joseph Criss and Supreme Court Justice Hertzfeld-Doll. The article came from a young reporter, trying to make a big name for herself, but clearly biting off more than she could chew. The name of that reporter, Rebecca Soundingham.

When this was brought to Katherine's attention, she simply laughed. After reading the article, she commented that Soundingham should give up journalism for creative writing, as her skills at creating fiction were well-tuned. Her lawyers, yes even Justices have lawyers, asked her if they should contact the author with a cease and desist order. Katherine said no and waved her hand at the matter, as though she was pushing a fly away. "No, it's not worth my time to worry over it. She's ruining her own credibility and I'm sure Joseph's lawyers are already there. His reputation is more at stake here, not mine. I won't do anything that will risk dragging the Supreme Court through the mud."

Sure enough, within the day a counter-article had been posted by Justin Ames (small world, eh?) pointing out the factual errors in Soundingham's story and refocusing on the economic issues at stake in the Criss Entertainment Holdings case.

A few weeks after that, the case was dropped completely. Apparently the legal team at CEH had fumbled their attempt to file a writ of certiorari. The case would go nowhere and CEH would be bound to the ruling of the Supreme Court of California, and thereby be required to pay taxes to their funny uncle every year.

By the end of the calendar year, Ames, who had broken the story, had a book deal. His topic? Joseph Criss and the Era of the Playboy Mogul. He evaluated the benefits given to CEOs like Criss because of their charm and good looks, but highlighted that their physical appearance would never compensate for a lack of business acumen. The feminists were ecstatic at a male-on-male attack on machismo corporate cultures.

Katherine and Ron were content to ring in another year together, unphased by the latest chapter in the weird tale that they had been dragged into. Joseph Criss started his year alone, insecure, and waiting for word from his accountants as to the total losses sustained from the recent stock sell-off. Rebecca Soundingham changed her major to Philosophy with an emphasis in Business Ethics. And, Helen Graham left Jay Karkowitcz.

She didn't want to be anyone's Dolly either.

ESCAPING AVILA CHASE

It was cold.

Or rather, it was cool. The morning air was just a shade below a comfortable temperature as I sauntered home along South Street. It was the afterglow of summer in Philadelphia where fall was just starting to loom in the early morning hours. The day would still be warm enough, but that morning was too cool for the t-shirt and jeans that I was wearing. The same that I had been wearing since the night before. Or, had only temporarily removed. Nonetheless, I was underdressed, a little exposed, and walking at a fast clip to make it back to my apartment so I could shower, shave, and get to the office on time.

I didn't often make a habit of going out to bars on work-nights, but the previous night had been a Sunday and I was stuck with the option of staying in and contemplating my current misery or going out to drown my sorrows in whiskey. I had chosen the latter. And as fortune would favor me, the evening had turned out to my benefit as a friendly woman of loose morals took me home for the evening. I was able to forget my troubles in her embrace. However, by morning, all of my worries had caught up to me, as though they were watching me through the unfamiliar apartment windows, begging for me to try and shut them out.

With each clop of my shoes on the concrete sidewalk, I retraced my thoughts and intentions, not only of the previous night, but of the previous decade. I was a man haunted and I could still feel that ghost hovering just behind me, beckoning me to turn around and confront my sins.

I passed the small bakeries that had delicious aromas steaming through the open doors, sandwich shops that wouldn't open until the afternoon, and tourist kiosks that became more prominent as I worked my way towards the Broad Street line.

My feet carried me quickly down the tiled stairs, through the turnstile, and onto the car heading north within seconds. My luck must have been keeping up with me. As the car trundled down the tracks, I took one of the empty seats and found myself staring at a gray and brown reflection of myself, only some of my features illuminated against the passing concrete walls of the subway system. My immediate thought was to notice how exhausted I looked. I was quick to remind myself that I was wearing the exhaustion of a man who had just gotten laid, so I tried to shrug off my continued feeling of self-loathing. That particular feeling would only creep up and crawl onto my skin whenever I thought about *her*. And that is exactly what I had been doing that morning. And the night before that. And the night before that.

It wasn't the girl who had taken me home that was on my mind. She was nice enough and pretty enough, but not anyone that I wanted to see again. Lenore, that was the name of the woman who had taken pity on me at the bar. She was kind and one-of-a-million bottle blondes with Tastykake padded thighs and an atrocious accent. She had given me her number earlier in the evening, but after a few more drinks she was desperately hinting as her willingness to take me home. I had inspected the scrap of paper with her phone number on it quickly as I had dressed that morning. Her twos were sloppy, excessively curvy and likely a little too indistinguishable. Her one begged for further clarification. It wasn't any "l" or "I" or numeral of some kind, but instead it was a resolute hash-mark. It looked like one of many days of a prison sentence. And her five must have usually been clear and distinct, but on this scrap of paper it only looked like an "s." I looked at the crumpled corner of a napkin that had been hastily ripped and written on, and re-crumpled it gently. With delicate precision I had placed it directly below where my jeans had hung across Lenore's kitchen chair, so that it would look as though it had accidentally fallen out. It would be an innocent enough reason for me to have 'lost' her number and completely remove my need to call or feel remorseful for not reaching out to her again.

I recall now that I had been smiling at this thought, pleased at my own little trick, when I looked up , through the subway window, and directly into the eyes of the one woman I was trying to forget the most. No surprise, there she was. Watching me, looking out at me as though I was on a wanted poster and she was studying my features so that she could report me at any second. But, she was the one on the poster. Those damned posters that had been up for two weeks now and had brought on my most recent bought of drinking and guilt-ridden sleepless nights.

Those piercing green eyes were at bus stops, in the windows at local shops, and generally all over the city. I could see her eyes judging me, as though she had summoned some hateful memory of me when the photo had been taken. Most other people would just recognize the eyes as female, clear green, and unyielding. They may even recognize their owner, most locals would. I'm talking, of course, about our latest Philadelphian sensation. A home-town girl who had made it big. The same one who left my heart under her boot heel in the process.

You would think that after almost a decade I'd be over it. She was the hardest one to get rid of and naturally, the one I just couldn't shake. That morning I should have been able to shake her from my mind, focus on the beginning of another busy work-week, and just plug-on without giving her another thought. But she was there. Haunting me as ever. Finally, the car pulled away and I stood, waiting for the next stop to rush out before the morning commuters really began to pile in.

Once I got off the subway, through the maze of hallways and stairs at 15th and Market, I made my way up through Dilworth Plaza and cut across to Walnut quickly. I walked up to 18th and turned quickly to enter my building. The chill of the morning was still stuck to my skin and I wanted to get inside before I started to get a runny nose.

In the shower I tried not to let my mind wander again. I couldn't afford a luxurious soul searching shower, I needed a quick rinse-down before heading to the office. I decided I could handle a little scruff and some smart-guy comments about the thin layer of gristle on my chin. Once I had changed into my suit, combed through my hair, and grabbed an apple, I felt the routine of Monday morning starting to settle in. I put on my black leather shoes, tied the laces quickly, and began to eat my apple as I strolled back down to the ground level and out into the morning. The sun was starting to warm the concrete. Something about that moment felt very peaceful to me. Maybe I was relieved to be wearing longer layers to keep myself warm since I hate to be cold. Maybe it was the natural sugar from the apple that was beginning to perk up my system. Maybe it was the after-effects of a pleasurable evening. I still haven't pinpointed what made me feel so good. But I do recall that I did feel very good, and that it was such a stark contrast to how I had felt before, and also after, that moment.

Because just as I was working my way through the familiar streets of my city, I was confronted, once again, with not only a poster, but a huge banner highlighting my worst fear.

Perhaps I should start to enlighten you as to my plight. I had been on the wrong end of a bad break-up many years earlier. Even though I had experienced some other failed relationships since then, likely stemming from my inability to get over this root-event, this particular romance had left a scar beyond measure. And the havoc it was wreaking was continuing to spill across new layers of my life. The messiest of all romantic ends was with Miss Avila Chase. Yes, the one with the Scarlet Moore paranormal mystery series. *Oh you've read them? You think they're just fantastic? Screw you.*

She may smile pretty for her interviews and press releases now, but I've seen the scowl that she hides. That hideous mug she makes when she cries. Followed by her face that gets pink with anger as her eyes turn from sea to crystalline green. She was so stubborn. She just had to win, she always had to be right. So I left her and just as I expected then, this icky, scratching, uncomfortable guilt has been with me for years. That feeling was subtle at first, but in the months leading up to that specific morning as I chewed my apple and hurried to work, it had blossomed into an unwieldy mass that I could not bear. My arms were spread out like Atlas trying to carry that heavy guilt, my legs quivering from the strain of it. Even with the early morning sun and my fresh apple, I could not escape the panic imposed by her memory.

What might cause this anxiety you ask? Well, her latest

novel, #10 in the series, was due to hit bookshelves at the end of that week. The series was an international hit and because she was from Philadelphia, my city, the city that she left when we were over, she was getting significant local attention. She was kicking off her book-tour with a large party and book signing that upcoming Friday. At the bookstore just down the block. The banner proclaiming the midnight release party was going up just as I was beginning to savor that brief and happy moment. I shook my head and pressed on.

At first, her books had gone unnoticed. Avila had signed on to a disadvantageous deal with a literary agent the year before we met. She cranked out her first masterpiece only to have it edited within an inch of its life and panned by all of the critics. She became convinced that if her work had not been shredded by the publishing house that it would have performed better. She found a way out of her contract and began to work on the second and third books in the series.

Enter me, Trevor Hobbertson. When we had first met and Avila explained that she was a writer of novels, I half expected her to confess that she wrote penny-store romance novels or erotic re-writes of popular fiction. I was relieved to know that her focus was on mysteries and the para-normal or super-normal, or hypo-normal.

Our relationship must have been fated to fail because when we met she was already involved with two others: *Scarlett Moore and the Invasion of the Hidden Tomb* and *Scarlett*

Moore and the Nirvana Paradox. Those books were her lovers, her something on the side of our relationship. At first, like in most relationships, it was pleasant and happy. I was so proud of her work and relished each opportunity she gave for me to proofread her latest chapters, scan for any continuity issues. I was her go-to guy.

Each book followed the adventures and mishaps of a museum curator turned paranormal activity detective: Scarlett Moore. Think female Indiana Jones meets X-Files. Avila was always such a history nerd; she poured so many nuanced details into each book. I would never admit this to anyone who asks me directly, but I think the stories are actually great. However, my official public position is that: "I don't much care for her little stories, same as I don't care for the doodles of strangers on coffee napkins."

But, I digress.

Each novel in the series revealed a new paranormal mystery. Intertwined into the subplot was Scarlett's love life, which always left something to be desired. There was also frequent reference to Scarlett's overly affectionate cat: Nibbles. Avila always tried to vary how much she played up these secondary lines. The first novel, *Scarlett Moore and the Wondrous Mystery of the Nile*, which I read after our second date so that I could ask her more about it, was perfunctory. I could see why Avila was so indignant with the publishing house. When we moved in together after 3 months of dating, she came with her clothes, shoes, pots, pans, and two boxes full of unsold copies of her debut novel.

It was easy then to be crushed for her. I took a box to work and pressured my coworkers into buying the book. I was like one of those obnoxious dads pushing Girl Scout cookies on their colleagues, only I was peddling for my girlfriend. To this day, I don't know if any of them read that book, and I don't care. I was a doting and attentive boyfriend. I understand that the description is entirely self-serving at this point, but it was true.

As the second and third books progressed, I helped her out as best as I could. However, a startling trend began to emerge in the secondary plot lines. In the first novel, Scarlett Moore was thrown into her first adventure when an overseas vacation with her then-boyfriend went a little haywire. Flash forward to the ending, the boyfriend was an international art smuggler. *Tisk tisk. Bad boyfriend.*

This began my torture and reverie. While enjoying a leisurely glass of wine one evening, Avila was telling me about her only trip abroad when she was still in college. She was flowing through some anecdote about how she lost a hat in St. Mark's Square in Venice when she abruptly ended her story. I was curious as to the sudden change.

"Well, then what happened?" I had asked so innocently, taking in my last swallow of Burgundy.

"Nothing, I bought a new hat. I think I actually lost it on another trip so maybe I should keep this up as a running in-joke." Avila brushed off her story quickly and I could see in her eyes that she didn't want me to ask any more questions. But of course, I did.

"So, were you there alone?" I finally hit a nerve

because her eyes darted around the room, searching for anything to fix on rather than look me in the eyes. She sipped on the wine in front of her, trying to look casual, but helplessly caught in my snare.

"No, I was with a friend," another sip of wine, a quick motion to get off the couch and refill my glass.

"Which friend?" I was being playful, I was being coy, I was being the irresistible self that had made her like butter in my hands so many times.

"Oh, you don't know 'em," she waved her hand as if she was swatting the question away like a mosquito. Her words were slightly hard to understand as she rushed through her answer and headed into the kitchen. But, I heard the one word she had tried to conceal the most.

"A 'him' is it?" I was in a playful mood; I wanted to see how uncomfortable this might make her feel. I pressed on.

"Yep," she said quickly. Her eyes were so focused on not meeting mine, it was so cute and funny, but a little worrisome. The more that she kept trying to push off her answer the more worried I became. "My ex, Anthony."

She had never mentioned her exes before, but neither had I. We hadn't gotten to the point of openly discussing our past relationships: what went wrong, what pet peeves we had inherited from them, what we blamed ourselves for in each messy end. Hearing his name for the first time was a little rattling.

I relented after I saw how uncomfortable she became. We finished our wine and discussed other topics. The thought kept picking at my synapses; begging for me to look deeper and find out why she had been so coy, so sealed about it that she had stopped mid-thought rather than let his name slip. Why had it taken so much prodding to find out this small detail?

Being the regular snoop that I am, I took a little time to search for this Anthony. I guess I could say 'well it is my job,' but none of my duties for the F.B.I. require or remotely imply that Facebook stalking my girlfriend's ex-boyfriend is part of the job. Surely, my many exes would have liked to be able to check up on my trail of failed attempts at monogamy before I met them. Oh well.

A quick search quickly revealed an 'Anthony Smith.' He was handsome and tan, but I wasn't feeling insecure because of his appearance. No, it was a thin line of text that began to play through my mind, as though Avila was reciting directly from her book:

It was the summer adventure of a lifetime with Aaron. Scarlett could hardly contain her giddy excitement at the idea of a European vacation with her college sweetheart. Would he propose? Would he drop to one knee, his thick black hair catching in the wind, his dark as night brown eyes twinkling with love? Scarlett could only imagine what her tanned and handsome boyfriend- perhaps fiancé- would look like as they savored each moment of their trip, and each evening with each other.

-Scarlett Moore and the Wondrous Mystery of the Nile

I couldn't help but compare the written description of the supposedly fictional Aaron and the real life Anthony Smith. Perhaps it was all a coincidence. Many men have dark hair, and dark eyes, and could tan in the summer. Pssh- nothing to worry about, I kept telling myself.

But, with each chapter that I helped to review for her subsequent novels, I could tell that the love interests for Scarlett were following an odd trend: they were horrible to her, they were untrustworthy, they were devastatingly handsome, and they all met a bad end either by law enforcement or an unsavory death by their own ignorance or negligence.

The last piece of the puzzle fell into place a month or so later. An off-hand comment from one of Avila's close friends at some party had sealed our fate. The truth that was revealed those many years ago had brought me to that present moment of despair and pained annoyance as I hurried to work, wiping away the juice that flowed from the apple onto my chin.

The comment that was made at the party had been innocent enough. This friend, whose name I can't even remember, was going on about how she was so happy that Avila had found me. This friend was so happy because Avila's most recent ex, Roman, had left her in a negative tailspin of a break-up. Sure enough, a quick search revealed a man by the same name. His picture matched the description of the Reginald Thompson that had been featured in the second and third installments of the Scarlett Moore novels.

I could have let it go. I should have let it go. But, I had to know more. As more time had passed, Avila and I had grown closer, our relationship more solid and established. I simply couldn't leave it alone. I wanted to understand what compelled her to do as I suspected, to write her ex-boyfriends into her novels. *Why couldn't she let it be? Was she unable of creating villains out of thin air? Did she use her reality as a crutch with which to craft her fiction? Would I become a story at a later date?*

One evening, after a homemade dinner, we stood in our small apartment kitchen. Me, cleaning the dishes, and Avila standing to my left waiting for wet dishes to dry. Our familiar routines were the comfortable knitting that started to warm my cold heart, but the fabric soon began to itch and irritate me. This was the first of many "itchings."

The conversation began innocently enough. "I think I am ready to start writing out my ideas for the next novel." She had only recently finished the manuscripts to the second and third Scarlett Moore stories and had mentioned that she needed a break from Scarlett for a bit.

"Oh yeah, where will Miss Moore be going this time?" I asked, genuinely curious as to what she would come up with this time. I was impressed by her creativity, something I will no longer admit to.

"I'm still taking a break from Scarlett. I think I want to write a murder-mystery." I could tell by her voice, the way she put a nervous emphasis on the second clause, that she was looking for some validation of her new endeavor. I couldn't deny that my own literary tastes were a bit more masculine: suspense, thriller, mystery. Technically women write in these genres as well, but I tend to find that I only prefer to read male authors.

"I'd like to read that," I was genuine and smiled at this. But, my next thought slipped out too quickly. "Although, I'd like to find out what happens with Scarlett and Roman." *Whoops*. I had been translating the text of her books in my mind, everywhere I saw the name 'Reginald', I was automatically thinking 'Roman,' and picturing the face that I had seen online. This was the first time that I had vocalized this thought and it was a mistake.

"What?" she reacted quickly.

"I mean Scarlett and Reginald," I was transparent, it was a foolish lie to tell. It must have been that soft fabric of our relationship beginning to nag and chaff.

"No, you said Roman." By now, she had placed the dish that was in her hands on the counter with extreme care, holding her composure as clearly as she could.

I hesitated to release the thoughts that I had been bottling up. Then, I let it out. "I know that you have been using your exes as characters in your books. I know how things ended with Anthony or should I say, Aaron."

"Oh, you know how things ended?" Her arms crossed and her eyebrows furrowed quickly. She was in her animalistic attack position.

"I know that you're still hung up on your ex-boyfriend, why else would you be writing him into your books?" I broke out into my Philadelphian ways, gesturing with my hands to emphasize my point, as though the cabinet that my hand was directed at somehow contained evidence to prove my point.

"That's not it at all, Trevor." She was calculated in her answer. She had more that she wanted to say, but she didn't let it slip.

"Oh really? Then why are you spending all this time having Scarlett go around and have these romances with Roman?!" I laid out the evil and green venom that was in me.

"What? I'm not Scarlett, Trevor. And Reginald isn't Roman. If you're jealous about some guy that I'm not with anymore, that's on you. If you want to talk through this, we can. But I'm not going to stand here and have you yell your paranoid theories at me." She started to walk away. I knew that I had lost because as much as I tried to play it cool, I was jealous.

"Okay, so what if I am jealous?" She had already moved into the living room, sitting on the patterned and faded sofa, facing away from me. I stood in the doorway between the kitchen and the living room. Not really in the same space as her, but not specifically in the other space. This would be the limbo I would learn to live in.

"Why? Things didn't end well with Roman; it's not like I'm hoping we'd get back together. And I'm with you!" I could see that she was shaken by what I was saying.

"Then why is your character described to look exactly

like him?" I knew she couldn't deny that.

She let out an exasperated sigh. I could see I had caught her in a thought, but then it must have shaken free from her because she turned her face quickly. "Wait, do you know Roman?"

"No, but I can do a Facebook search, Avila." I was moving closer to her; I didn't like the forced space between us.

"You've been stalking my ex-boyfriend on Facebook?" She was only getting more frustrated. I was stubborn and had to prove my point.

"Oh, like you haven't gone through my old photos and tried to see what my ex looked like?" She didn't respond to that one.

"Why-," she changed sentences while speaking, "where is this all coming from?" She was rubbing the spot right between her eyebrows; was she really getting a headache from this conversation? That motion was her tell, or maybe she was just playing me. I wouldn't put it past her, now that I have hindsight to better inform my memory. She could have been feigning a headache just so that I would drop the subject.

"I can read Avila. If you're writing your ex into your novel, then you clearly aren't over him." I tried to emphasize my point once again with my hands. It didn't seem to help my argument in the end.

"But I am. If I wasn't, I wouldn't be able to still talk to him." She said it as though these words were supposed to soothe me somehow.

It took me a moment to compose my next thought. "Wait, you still talk to Roman? Like on a regular basis?"

"Yes, we're friends." Avila looked at me like I had just asked her what year it was or who the president was, as though I was an uninformed time traveler hoping to catch-up with a temporal loop.

"How close of friends? You haven't mentioned hanging out with him once since we've been together?" Now I felt like an interrogator, I needed to know the details so that I could assess the situation fully.

"I talk to him a couple of times a year. We just keep in touch, that is all." She shrugged off this piece of information as thought it was so casual and banal.

"Well, why? Things are over and done between the two of you, why keep in touch?"

"That is oversimplifying things. We've shared some hard times together, he's the only other person that understands that tragedy. We can't shut each other out." Avila acted as though I had suggested not breathing oxygen for an extended period. Or as if I had implied that she could easily spend a week walking on her hands. The absurdity of my words were apparent on her face.

"Why don't you try me? I can try to understand you; I can work to be that person for you." I was pleading, and this, quite clearly now, was the point of fracture.

"I don't see why you're so upset over my fictional characters and now you're upset over my friends?"

"I'm upset that you write these hot scenes between two fictional characters that seem a lot like you and your ex, Roman. And I'm frustrated that you have been all buddy-buddy with him without telling me." Honesty, while it may be advertised as refreshing, is often just a noxious as bleach. Honesty was ripping us apart. It is effective, but at what cost?

"Don't you trust me?" My recollection of the soft way that she spoke those words would galvanize my resolve in the moments that I would experience later on, as I slithered from one relationship to the next.

"I do, but,- " I was about to just come right out and say it, and I did. "What is more important to you? Our relationship, or your friendship with Roman?"

She had given me the answer that I wanted at the time, but within the next four months, we were finished. Being friends with Roman was more important to her. That might not have been the final straw for her, but it was the first of many to snap and shift the weight on our backs.

So, why did any of this matter as the world prepared for her latest novel? My ex-girlfriend wrote her books about her ex-boyfriends, whether she would admit it or not. Big deal, right?

Well, as you know, she started a rapid-fire publishing schedule about ten years ago (the year after we split). This allowed her to shoot to the top of every best-seller list. I couldn't turn any corner, or scroll through a news feed without seeing her, or a reference to her books, or the upcoming movie deals. Then abruptly, two years ago, there was only silence. Not a prose piece, not a book review, not an interview, nothing. It was the most peaceful time I had ever experienced.

Until that summer, when her publicity juggernaut started up again. The latest novel by Avila Chase would be released at the end of that week. All of my educated deduction skills indicated that I would be featured in this fiction. I hadn't been adapted into a character in her other novels, surely this new novel would be the one where she decided to cast me as the villain. I had been agonizing over how she would depict me. Would she state that some mysterious and ultimately evil man had "muted blue eyes with flecks of steely grey?" or would she refer to my "uniquely metered swagger" and the "loping swing of my gate"? I might be called out by the description of my hair, "blonde and matted, flopping on the top of my head at a playful angle," or the "harsh contrast of hallowed dark bags under my eyes." Perhaps she might only make allusions to me by calling out my "jolting habit of cracking my knuckles with loud and distinct pops," or my "unfortunate and untimely allergy" to the most ridiculous of fruits.

The constant speculation was draining. I waned and waxed like the phases of the moon between denial, acceptance, and hopeless bargaining with my unconscious mind. It made me wish that whiskey in my morning coffee wasn't frowned-upon. It was shaping up to be one hell of a Monday.

By the time I had arrived at the office, swiped my security badge, and made it through the maze of desks to my cubicle, I was going through the motions of the day and was already beginning to forget the colorful start to my morning. As my standard-issue computer booted, I grabbed my trusty mug and headed to the break room for coffee where there was, as usual, a small group of other agents and admins loitering as they waited for the latest pot to finish brewing. I did the math quickly and six people waiting for coffee with a four-cup machine would put me at least another 20 minutes out from a fresh cup. I headed back to my desk and figured that if I really needed the pick-me-up, I would head back to the break room in a bit. Given my level of stress, lack of sleep, and all around miserable demeanor that day, I really should have waited for the coffee. The dopamine drip of the caffeine into my system would have assuaged the headache that was setting in.

The headache was the result of a long-established morning routine in which I consumed a moderate amount of caffeine, my minor hangover, and the recently developed habit of grinding my teeth at night. The habit was actually a resurrected behavior. It began in those final months with Avila and persisted for the following year. Without really trying, it abated and had lied dormant until the announcement of the new book, Scarlett: Avenged.

While I was distracting myself from the throb of my headache and the various contributing factors, I began to thumb through the top files on my desk. I had been successful in completely forgetting about work over the weekend and needed a bit of a jog on my memory. *Ah, right, gift card fraud.*

You may scoff at the idea, but where there is the opportunity for money to change hands, there is always the opportunity for fraud. I had been working a solid stream of gift card fraud since that previous spring. As the seasons of that year evolved, I began to develop a knack for identifying and putting an end to significant operations.

When I tell people that I work for the FBI, I can see that their minds fill with pictures of secret missions, bullet proof vests, drawn hand-guns, and unnecessary danger. I was relegated, however, to the Financial Crimes division. When I began working for the Bureau, I was assisting on insurance fraud cases and other white-collar crimes. Having been able to develop a penchant for cracking electronic funds fraud, I was able to make myself a little niche. Work had been steady, and while others in law enforcement may wish for a day when people would just obey the laws and stop causing trouble, I didn't mind the job stability.

What I had been able to identify was the two main abuses for these gift cards. I'm not talking about $25 to iTunes or even $100 to Outback Steakhouse. The main cards that are used for fraud are certain kinds of the American Express or Visa gift cards. They work just like a debit card, but they have a fixed amount. You have a relative who needs money? Buy one of these cards and put on the amount they need; you pay a small processing fee, but you have some protection as long as you save the activation codes. Once the money is spent, the person can get rid of the card or refill it. Most people use them innocently enough.

The first main area for excessive use and re-use are the credit-card churners. They are hungry for travel rewards miles and purchase the gift cards on their shiny new plastic to meet the bonus point thresholds within the short time given. The churners use the gift cards to pay their bills, groceries, anything. Some are able to transfer the money back to their bank accounts to be able to pay for the credit card bill. In all, the churners lose the five-dollar transaction fee with each card. Technically, nothing illegal was done. But, credit card companies were starting to catch on. The hay-day of churning was drawing to an end. While that method abuses the system, these churners were making the most of open loopholes and it was not illegal, so they were all good by me and Bureau.

The area that I was focusing on was the small time thieves that were preying on dear granny, or anyone naïve enough to hand over cash for a gift card, without asking too many questions. Did you ever hear a story like this twenty or so years ago? A friend, an acquaintance, or just a person on the street says that they need cash. They have lost all of their credit cards and as odds would have it only have their checkbook on them. Because not all stores will accept a check, they are in a bind, but they swear that they are good for the money. The gullible party hands over their cash in exchange for a check that would bounce.

Well, with these gift cards the party that is "in-a-bind" is handing over a gift card in exchange for cash and making off with the money. Because these cards can hold up to $500, the opportunity to thieve was great. The criminals that I had caught were smart and only claimed between $80 and $150 at a time. They would hand over the gift card with a proof of purchase and take off with the cash. The illegal part comes in when the criminal hands over a forged receipt with a fake activation code and incorrect information on the activation fee.

My current file, which I had begun working on a month earlier, revealed a tricky new twist. The smarter criminals were just taking the forged activation codes and finding a way to manipulate the system to allow them to activate the cards. A lot of computer code and cracking was involved. As one of my IT friends had explained: Hackers are good, Crackers are bad. Hackers seek to point out back doors and weak points in code; Crackers seek to exploit these breaks for their own gain. The Crackers were finding a way to activate the gift cards, transfer the money to an online account to purchase items, or just reload their online payment accounts. The systems were catching on within 20 minutes of fraudulent activity, so the thieves had to cover their tracks quickly. They were forced to virtually launder the money. Many were funneling the money through innocuous websites that likely had no idea that their pages were being used for such nefarious activities.

The majority of the transactions were run through the RF server. Yes, the popular and often imitated RF server had been used in all of this. The first, of now many, self-service web-hosting companies was Roman's Forum, now abbreviated to RF. The founder, Roman, who had started out by offering up his free webpage codes in online forums, was just trying to be helpful and pass the time while he was bored at his desk job. He finally got funding and launched the WYSIWYG platform that allows just about anyone to sign up and start a website for free, with advanced design and analytics options for a monthly subscription fee. He was a genius and now WordPress, Squarespace, Wix, and all of the others in the market were trying to copy the model.

The one item that often brought the founder, Roman, praise was that he headquartered his company in Philadelphia. He brought tech jobs to the city and managed to staunch the flow of the post-graduate brain-drain from Philadelphia colleges and universities.

The downside is that this guy, Roman, was that he is the same one that I referenced earlier. That's right, in this case, all roads lead back to Avila. My latest case involved a cracker who was funneling laundered money through Roman's Forum. I had been avoiding direct and even indirect interaction for a while. The first few instances involved sloppy criminals and a multitude of websites that didn't go through the RF server.

My latest file was on a criminal that had found a way to massage and manipulate the RF server so that he had a longer time window to launder his digital money. In my mind, this was a stupid criminal because he was using the same paths over and over again. It was as if he wanted to get caught. Nevertheless, this also meant that I had to seek the cooperation of Roman's Forum to be able to provide evidence on the user and close the case. *Was there a deeper conspiracy at hand? Did this criminal somehow know of my weak spot, my aversion? Perhaps they were smarter than I thought.*

My headache was starting to dig in. I rubbed my head to try and convince it to stop hurting.

At the end of that long Monday, I felt that I had made a significant accomplishment. I was one fifth through that week that would get more difficult every day as the book launch approached. My sanity was still mostly intact and I had been fairly productive at work in spite of my tourettic habit of pitying myself and ruminating on my hatred of Avila. After a good workout, a lousy dinner, and a mind-numbing hour of television, I was ready for sleep. I had taken an over-the-counter sleep aid and washed it down with some water, fresh and fluoridated.

Against my better judgment, I continued to watch TV. I thought that once the pill kicked in, I could really exhaust myself if I fought the urge to sleep. Yes, I do tend to follow the advice that I give myself, even if it makes no sense.

My eyes lolled between the TV screen and the empty walls of my apartment. As my thoughts wandered from the weak plot line of the show and began to focus on my immediate surroundings, I became fixed on thoughts of my apartment. The walls were empty and bare, as would be expected of any young bachelor.

I wasn't that young anymore, though. There were pockets of furniture between wide expanses of open floors. There was a wasteland, a wilderness, of empty space in the apartment where dust clumps would form and stick to the floorboards. I hadn't ever really settled in, but I was somehow ingrained to this threadbare space. I could always excuse the appearance by giving a line about consumerism and trying to appear as though I was deliberately keeping my space clean and my possessions to a minimum. Really, I was just too apathetic and lazy to make a solid decision. I was too caught in my own past to ever really settle in, but I was also too committed in my hope for a happy future to accept that I needed a massive change in my life.

I should have been living out in Manayunk, but instead I stayed in the heart of the city. I should have been living the life that the rest of my generation was so keen to post and share with ease. But I was trapped, I was shut-off, and I couldn't stop lying to myself. It was just so easy at that point to continue the rouse.

The show ended and the blaring theme of the news report caught my attention. I snapped back to reality and looked at the TV, forgetting all self-pitying thoughts of my inner turmoil being manifested in my undecorated apartment.

As the nightly news faded into comedy re-runs, I heard my cell phone buzz. From the comfort of my couch I looked around to see where I had left it in the apartment. There was a soft glow from the kitchen and I heard the buzz again. I calculated the effort required to stand up and walk the few feet to the kitchen counter. It seemed an insurmountable feat at the time. My muscles and joints were succumbing to the effects of the sleeping pill; I was weighted down with chemical lead in my veins.

After the second distinct buzz there was silence. In that silence, I contemplated my pathetic position of being too lazy to get up and answer my own phone. I bullied myself into standing and made the three-second journey to the other side of my apartment. I palmed the phone and swiped to access my home screen. The compact and innocuous yellow icon that led to my text messages had a bright red circle in the upper right hand corner with the number "2" on it. This indicated that I had not one, but two messages awaiting my response. The small joys of lonely adulthood include getting two text messages on a weeknight. *Hooray!* I thought in my exhausted state.

I opened up the messages, both were from Nick. My good ole buddy Nick who never kept in touch, or called, or made plans to get drinks, or offered a spare Phillies ticket, or made any attempt to contact me unless Avila was involved. We had been great friends. During the time that Avila and I were together we were "couple-friends" with Nick and his then-girlfriend. Nick had been a very chill guy and was dating one of Avila's good friends. We grouped together at parties, we went on double dates, the girls chatted in the kitchen while Nick and I watched the Birds on Sunday nights. It was a cozy view of domesticated life and I suspect that Nick and I would have remained closer if his then-girlfriend, now wife, Claudette, hadn't sided with Avila. I lost the girl and the associated friends in the split, but at least I got to keep the city.

After it all ended, Avila left town, but Claudette and Nick stayed loyal to her. Nick had sent me text messages for a while asking how I was and tried to make an effort, as though he wasn't completely whipped by Claudette.

When Avila's novels were released, he would send an email asking how I had been and giving some perfunctory life updates. Within one or two responses, he would usually steer the conversation to Avila and the latest book. Nick was aware of the trend that I had detected in her novels, I had told him my theory as the relationship was imploding. While he may have been elusive and absent as a friend most of the time, he did remain true to me in one aspect. Nick would read Avila's novels, as Claudette would expect him to, but he would keep an eye out for any romantic references. Nick would send me chunks of text with the simple note: "don't know if this means you or not, but figured you would be curious."

He actually kept the same text in his emails with each subsequent release. I began to suspect that he was just copying and pasting from one email to the next. It was a CRTL-ALT-Friendship, but he did help me through the anguish I was feeling. I could picture him making notes in the margins and dog-earring pages so that he could reference them again as he peered over and copied one sentence at a time into his emails. How dedicated he must have been to the task. Perhaps he had been a better friend to me in all of this than anyone else, perhaps he had been better to me than I had been to myself.

Unfortunately, none of the passages that he sent meant much to me. I had read them through quickly, acting as though I didn't care. Later, I would meticulously study the text in the insomnia hours that followed. As you might have suspected when Avila's books went silent, so did Nick.

That evening his simple messages of, "Hey man" and then "How have you been?" were like the sound of an expected drumbeat. It felt like the tension released as the Tchaikovsky cannons were fired. I expected it. I knew it was coming, but it still rattled me each time and was followed by the period of familiar unease. *What if he stumbled across the passages written about me this time?*

As I stared at the text messages, I thought back to the most haunting passages he had sent me yet. I couldn't see myself in any of them. I tried to force myself into the descriptions, but it never worked. Avila hadn't written me in, yet. But some of her words started to get under my skin. I realized what true darkness was within her and wondered at how she must have transformed, transmorphed into some kind of twisted woman. Like this one:

"My long strands, gray beneath, but died brown then black then auburn, will cling to the small hairs on your arms, stick in the crook of your elbow like spider-webs and creep you out each and every time one slithers from the baseboards and up your body."

-Scarlett Moore and the Missing Volcano

So weird, right? Or this one:

"Does the orange and freshly oxygenated blood on my hands appease you? Should I mutilate myself some more? Should I scratch through another layer of skin on my palms and grind them into the gravel to be worthy of your touch?"

-Scarlett Moore and the Embargo of Eden

The plots of the Scarlett Moore novels were becoming progressively darker. The descriptions were becoming more eerie and warped. Was Avila crumbling under the pressure? Was it the result of something dark planted within her that was starting to take root? Were the grotesque depictions a result of her desire to seek retribution on me? It had occurred to me that she may have just enjoyed writing in that style, but that left my ego unappeased.

I locked my phone without responding to Nick and placed it face-down on the kitchen counter where it had been idling. I sauntered back to the couch trying to convince myself that I wasn't distracted by the memory of that. Based on her last novel, that dark matter in her of the dark passages that Avila had penned and that Nick had transcribed. I watched the remainder of a B-rated sitcom rerun that barely managed to keep my attention.

I felt the groggy haze of the sleeping pill starting to take hold, even though my mind was wildly active. Each synapse and cognitive function was trying to pull up those selected passages and work at deciphering them again. My memory was searching for some previously undiscovered clue, some hint as to the revenge Avila was undoubtedly plotting against me.

The show ended and I turned the television off. I was out-of-whack and so desperately wanted this mania to end, but I could see no way out of it now. I silently hoped for a night of dreamless sleep as I picked up my cell phone on the way to my bedroom. As my routine dictated, I set my phone to be charged, checked my alarm, and shuffled into the bathroom to brush my teeth and wash my face. I ran through the motions quickly and without thought, but my mind was still active. The servers in my 1,000-computer brain were whirring, spinning, and just getting started for the night.

As I settled into bed, I tried to focus on my denial.

Maybe she'll never write me in. Perhaps she had written it all out in some other story but refused to publish that work. Or perhaps she has cut out and braided each line into a thick rope that she will use to hang me.

Avila would find that appropriate. The monstrous vision of Avila I had constructed in my mind was capable mind had exploded outward. I wouldn't put it past her now. She was a femme fatale with creative license, and she was sharpening her pen just for me.

After a restless evening I climbed out of my own bed and started my morning routine. A quick shower, then a shave. It was slightly more painful because I had an extra day's worth of stubble on my chin. I recall the stubborn burn of the blade as it tugged, and pulled, and finally cut the short hairs on my jaw line. Like everything that week, it was drawn-out and painful.

I had settled in at my desk, with a fresh cup of coffee, and flipped through my usual links to check the news, log in to the requisite systems, and then finally to review the flags in the system for any fraudulent activity. Like a bright and shining star, there was another transaction by this latest fraudster, he went by the handle: Traveler. Usually he opted for some derivation of the word in his moniker: +R@v3l3r, or T®a<ele®, or some mixture of symbols and letters that spelled out the same word: Traveler.

This guy was actually very good at what he was doing. He had once again enabled a gift card with a fake activation code, found a way to arbitrage the currency through several websites, and was off with the money in 5 minutes. Once again, all of the sites were hosted through Roman's Forum and it appeared that he had used the same websites multiple times.

I shook my head at that last detail. I wanted to respect

this man for his ingenuity. If I could respect him and his criminal acuity then I could think like him, get in his head, and try to predict his next move. But I couldn't respect how lazy he was. *Was he trying to get caught?* It is an established fact within the cracking world that you don't use the same path more than once, and here this Traveler was flaunting his indifference to even his own criminal code. Did he have no respect for anything?

I might have called out to my desk-mate to say, "can you believe this guy?" or some similar remark. But, my most recent neighbor had been transferred to Pittsburgh and the cube next to mine was starkly empty. The carpets were beige, the cubicle walls were beige, and even the ambient noises gave off an overall mood of beige.

The office was quiet and everyone was keen to keep their heads down and get their work done. Except for the din of office white noise, there was no noise to catch my attention away from my thoughts. What I recall most about that week was the silence, the rattling and overwhelming silence from the real world. I was left to contend with the voices in my head far too often. Usually, this was great for me, but that week it was a torture. The isolation made things worse.

With this latest transaction, Traveler was up to over $76,000 in laundered funds. I needed to act quickly before he hit a major milestone number, like $100,000, and disappear into the refuge of an island nation with no extradition laws.

I went through the process of cataloging the

transaction and added it to a report I had already started. The additional details confirmed the pattern, the laundering process, and that the Traveler (I had to refer to him as "the suspect" in the report for official purposes) would likely do this several more times before taking off with the money. My number one recommendation was to ask Roman's Forum for access to their logs so that we could accurately verify the identity of the suspect. We had the I.P. addresses that had been used to access the funds, but most crackers were able to mask their I.P. address, so it did us little good. We needed the logs from RF to confirm the final destination of the funds and trace that back to the actual identity and location of the Traveler. He might not even be within Philadelphia city limits. This guy could be operating out of a basement in Utah. He could in fact be a world traveler. We couldn't know until we found the end of that trail.

I debated disclosing my connection with Roman in the report. Each time I began to type out the explanation, it seemed more and more ridiculous.

"We have a past lover in common…"

"He dated my ex-girlfriend before I did…"

"I can only assume that he knows who I am and holds an unwarranted animosity towards me…"

"He may not even know who I am, but I know who he is and it could get weird…"

I deleted each thought before it was completed. No need to make any mention of it at all. I had no evidence to suggest that Roman Trecki was knowingly abetting criminal activity on his server. He likely didn't know the day-to-day minutia of each user and link accessed. There was no plausible reason for me to implicate him and no grounds for it. I wasn't so out of whack over Avila that I would knowingly incriminate an innocent man.

I didn't want my fear over a perceived bias to mask any potential criminal activity. I was good at my job and was set against letting Avila have a hold over me at work as well. I needed to start building up a firewall against her in my mind. She may be ramming the gates of my life with her forthcoming novel, but I had to keep my workplace the bastion of sanity and professionalism. At least, those were my best intentions.

I finished my report and shot it over to my Director via email. Like a good agent, I awaited his approval on my proposed plan of action.

After a few minutes, I performed the habitual motion. The ritualistic check. From the Facebook homepage it was easy to navigate. The past searches populated the instant I typed the letter "A."

The Avila Chase fan page always displayed first on the list. The picture was unchanged; Avila was laughing with a sly smile. Perhaps it was a genuine candid, but likely it was a staged photo. By the look of the background she was at some event.

The second result was her actual personal page. The bright blue check mark next to her name indicated that it was her official page and genuinely belonged to her. I clicked and saw the same message that I had seen each time I had checked in the previous years. "This user's profile has been disabled. Please check back later."

I knew that if she really had disabled her account that her personal profile wouldn't have populated at all in the search. Had she blocked me perhaps? Maybe she had such a following on social media that she could retain her personal profile, but still allow it to appear disabled to those she wasn't friends with.

I clicked the bright red "X" in the top corner of the internet browser window and hurriedly clicked onto anything else. An old tax file popped up on my screen. What did that famous statesman, so well-known in Philadelphia, once say? "Nothing in life is certain except for death and taxes." Perhaps Ben Franklin omitted heartache from his list because he never knew Avila Chase.

The cover design for Scarlett: Avenged had been revealed earlier that summer with an alternative design. The primary cover art was the staring, cold eyes of Avila, likely used because she herself strongly resembled the written description of Scarlett. This was the image that I found myself constantly confronting throughout the city. Each day it was as though she was brow-beating me into a state of deranged paranoia.

The alternative design, probably what she and her publishing team expected would be used for the inevitable movie poster, didn't offer me much relief. The second design was a graphic of the Hindu god, Kali. The blue-skinned figure with multiple arms was facing away from the viewer and appeared to have long and flowing red hair, instead of the traditionally depicted black hair. As if I hadn't pictured, on multiple occasions, Avila coming after me with her animal hands trying to claw out my eyes and smother me with the weight of her fury. The alternate design was terrifying to me on so many new levels.

When I stepped out of the building for lunch that Tuesday afternoon, I was sick of my poor self-control and inability to focus. It was the worst possible week for an Avila Chase distraction, I wanted to catch the Traveler. I was thinking of his odd actions and potential motives as I strolled a block or so to reach my favorite spot for lunch. The air was clean and temperate. I could breathe easily and enjoyed seeing the streets of the city busy with other 9-to-5-ers resting on ledges and benches to enjoy their lunches.

I quickened my pace and managed to avoid slipping on the grease spots in the street as I jaywalked to the best spot for lunch in town. This place was an alley featuring a bank of food trucks that offered every kind of cuisine. They were busy that day, as each truck had a decent line for food.

There were medical professionals in mint green scrubs, chatting amongst themselves; an endless sea of pens, and clips, and id badges pouring out of their top breast pockets. There were women in heels and binding professional ensembles that made me think that they must be uncomfortable. There were other men in suits who had eschewed their blazers as they stood in line, they held them over their shoulders with one hand. A pose that they had likely seen in a catalog.

It was a perfect Philadelphian afternoon. People were out and about, the city was alive and bustling. Each person was moving like a blood cell in an intricate system, keeping the pulse of the city beating.

Oh, Philadelphia. The city that will remain loyal to you, so long as you remain loyal to it. It was a close family-member that was always there. It was the warm embrace that I felt every time I caught the sunset refracting off of the Cira Center. It was the romanticized notions that stirred up as I passed the outdated long-boats at Penn's Landing. If I could only keep one thing in my relationship with Avila, I'm glad that I kept this city.

I went to my favorite Chinese food truck and put in an order of sesame chicken and lo mein with a Coke. It was a five-dollar deal that you just couldn't beat. As I dawdled while my order was being prepared, I wondered about how the Traveler might be maneuvering. I wandered a few feet as I ran through the information on the case in my mind. I stopped in front of a newsstand and leaned against the brick wall that was behind me. Once I had cycled through the clues mentally, I entertained myself by perusing the headlines in front of me.

One particular item caught my eye. I saw the intricate Kali/Scarlett design on the cover of *Philadelphia Magazine*.

The story headline revealed that an interview with her was, in fact, the premier editorial for that month.

I picked up the magazine without even thinking and flipped through to the article. I tried to scan quickly, as though I was just a casual customer considering a purchase. I knew that I couldn't buy the magazine, though. It would be another means of torture to remind myself of my imminent doom. I found the interview.

The feature took up five pages, three of text and two of images. Avila was featured in profile in full make-up and hair blown-out. She was styled to look so glamorous. *How could they all not see how devious she was? How could people not see how hell-bent she was on destroying any man who dared to not love her forever?* I could see her as the man-eater that she was, though. I flipped through her answers quickly.

The interview was by the lead entertainment and events editor for the magazine, Dan Dorr, whose initials are listed as "DD" for reference:

DD: Avila, your work is technically categorized as science fiction because Scarlett focuses on out-of-this world phenomenon. But, each novel has an underlying message. What is the main focus for Scarlett: Avenged?

AC: Scarlett may be investigating paranormal activities, but it is always human errors that bring her back into this world. I wanted to focus on an issue that is important not just to women, but to society. We can't just say this is a woman's issue anymore, it's a human issue. Through Scarlett I can bring this problem to the forefront of our consciousness and hopefully spur change.

DD: And what inspired this specific message? This is your most outspoken work to date.

AC: What inspires anything? A personal connection, an experience that shifted my world view. It has taken some time to put my head around it, but I can see clearly that I need to take action and bring this to light. '

My stomach began to churn. Was this it? Was this the moment when she would reveal me as the negative focal point, the demon waiting in the wings, that had driven her creativity and success? I wasn't reading anymore. I was scanning ferociously. There were some references to Calcutta and a trip to Nepal. Blah, blah, blah.

Then, at the end of the interview was an excerpt from the novel. Out of place and out of context, I had no way to tell for sure what it referred to, but it left me spooked:

I envision your fist punching me, my fist punching you. My head slamming into your face, my oversized and unadorned forehead causing your front teeth to rip and pull from their gums. And each time, I see you holding up a bloody tooth, slimy with saliva. Your hand receives the blood as well, but the pulp of your teeth are not pink or even red like the fluids spilling from the sucking hole in your mouth. No, the pulp of your teeth, the fleshy matter that had once held it in, is like a thick patch of seaweeds. Flowing and breathing in the air, roots as white as your tooth, the remainder of the pulp is black. Inky black like an octopus, a slippery squeezing suffocating octopus. It's just like you, that is what you are.

-Scarlett: Avenged

At the sight of those words my hands twitched, releasing the magazine, letting it fall onto the grimy sidewalk. I picked it up quickly, crushing it in my hands. I tried to casually place it back on shelf. The pages were bent and crumpled. I couldn't steady myself or keep my hands from making a mess. The newspaper stand owner called out to me, "Stop fooling around and buy it already!" The men and women nearby looked at me with disdain. I was the interrupter of the idyllic peace that they were enjoying as they waited for their fast food. I was the crazy man, crouched on the ground, fumbling for papers, reminding them how fragile sanity can be.

I couldn't find the words in my throat to answer. I shook my head and wobbled away. I almost forgot my lunch order, but happened to pause to catch my breath as I heard my name called out in a heavy accent. I felt as though I was a wanted criminal, on the run, hiding in plain sight, and my cover was just blown by a clear and crisp wanted photo. Was everyone around me looking at me because I was sweating profusely, even though the weather was lovely? Were they worried that I was sick? Or perhaps, my secret was not so secret at all? Could there be some way for people to know my connection to Avila? Some kind of literary gossip scene that would clearly point the finger at me as the inspiration of her latest villain, her greatest villain yet based on the words in her interview?

Was the older woman, peering at me over the top of her fuchsia glasses, with her brightly dyed auburn hair, judging me? Did she know my secret? Was she reading my thoughts? Did she know my sins just by taking one look at me?

I wasn't even hungry anymore, but I brought my lunch back to my desk. I began to compulsively check online one more time. This time I typed in my own name and found no connections to Avila Chase on the first three pages of the Google Search Engine Results. Thank goodness for that.

I ate my lunch in silence. I could have gone into the breakroom and struck up a conversation with any person passing by, but I elected for my solitude. When it came time to open up my fortune cookie, I couldn't do it. I had tempted fate enough for one day. Besides, I had an overwhelming feeling that the tiny slip of paper would have lottery numbers to match Avila's birthday and that the fortune would read: "*Scarlett: Avenged*, by Philadelphia's daughter Avila Chase available this Friday!"

Avila was indeed my future; I was being pushed towards that fate every second.

"Good work, Hobbertson."
Those three words were my salvation on that Tuesday. They brought me out of my post-lunch hated-fueled panic.

My Director had called me into his office. He was well into his fifties with a paunch that constantly tugged at his shirts, the fibers appearing more and more tired with every second that passed. He was a good man. I will stand by that assessment to this day. Randy Knight is a good man. A wife and three kids with a McMansion out in Yardley, he was the mild-mannered and even-tempered FBI Director that you would hope to see. Not so driven by ambition as to be ruthless, but not so aimless as to sit by idly without taking action.

"Thank you, sir." I accepted my praise standing, watching Knight as he put the file containing my report back down onto his desk.

"Make contact with this Forums website today if you can. If your suspect is moving fast, he may wrap things up by this weekend. Why not? Am I right?"

"Yes, sir. Their headquarters are actually adjacent to City Hall, so I planned to drop in tomorrow morning before coming into the office."

"Great. Just in case they aren't as open and willing to help, have the warrant ready. These tech companies act so touchy when we ask for help. We want to catch criminals; why are we being treated like the bad guys because we are asking for specific information?" Knight shrugged and shook his head, it was clear that he was censoring a much longer diatribe that was still running through his mind.

I agreed with each word he had said, nodding along as he spoke.

"What am I telling you this for? You know it!" He patted the folder as though it were a small and precocious child. Knight had that odd habit. "Alright, Hobbertson, good work." I gave a curt nod and slipped out of his office.

I had never pictured myself as a 'yes-man' or a 'company-man.' But I did find comfort in being told that I was doing good work, in having my efforts recognized. I had been in an existential funk after things ended with Avila. I had spent years trying to get over her and I had found that the most effective method was to channel my energy into my work. That week I was experiencing the clawing effects of a relapse. Working hard and performing at my job kept me focused and grounded. It reminded me that I was one of the good guys, no matter what Avila thought or wrote about me.

I sat back in my chair and dialed the main number of RF. After an onerous phone tree and some hipster wait music, I finally spoke with a receptionist. She informed me politely that Mr. Trecki was absolutely booked and couldn't take any appointments. Once I clarified who I was and the reason for my meeting request she put me on hold. I felt a surge of power knowing that my title: "Special Agent" and employer: "The Federal Bureau of Investigation" aka "The Federal Bureau of Look At My Badge, Get Out Of My Way" would clear a path for me. I tried not to become addicted to that feeling, because it can be intoxicating. But, I enjoyed that sensation of power and control as the receptionist took me off of hold and informed me that Mr. Trecki would be able to meet with me first thing the following morning.

"Thank you, I will be in at 9 am," I said politely, as though I hadn't just played the trump-card in this situation.

"Excellent. We look forward to seeing you then." The receptionist cut the line after her overly cheery salutation. In that moment, I felt good. I felt in control. I knew that I had no ability to influence Avila, to persuade her to cease her mental torture, but I sure could get a lowly receptionist to jump at my command. That did feel good.

While I would have reclined at my desk for an extended period and basked in the glory of a job-well-done, I had plans that evening. I had plans every Tuesday evening. It was 10k Tuesday. I was part of the local run-club that would meet up and run through the city. We would meet at Philadelphia Runner at 16th and Sansom and head for the Schuylkill River Park, then follow that path up to the Art Museum. Some of the faster runners would add the steps to their run, after looping around to the front while waiting for the slower runners to catch-up, before heading down the parkway to Logan Square and back to the run-shop. Of course, we had to have drinks afterwards. We were young and upwardly mobile millennials. We would do just about anything that seemed like an accomplishment if it meant we could go drinking afterwards.

While we had discussed varying our run route and trying a different bar each week, we usually settled into the same route and almost always ended up at The Happy Rooster.

That week was no different. I left work at 5pm sharp. I had informed Knight of my weekly run-routine and he approved heartily. He would occasionally come up to my desk at 4:45 pm on Tuesdays and make small talk just so he could say, "Oh, would you look at the time. You've gotta get going if you want to make your run club."

I couldn't tell if he was being sincere or if he just wanted to feel somehow included. I had invited him to join us once or twice. He never took me up on the offer. For a man with a sedentary lifestyle, I think just saying the word "run" got his heart rate elevated for the recommended 30 minutes.

That week I had my computer shut down and my desk cleaned right on time. I slipped out quietly and headed home. Most nights I would stay until 6:30 or 7:00 pm with the other agents. I didn't sense any animosity from them because of my weekly indulgence, but I still didn't try to make a big thing of it. I waved to Director Knight as he came out of his office and caught my eye.

After a brisk walk home and a change into my running clothes, I grabbed a banana and a cool bottle of water, then headed to meet the group. My previous routine had consisted of running only on the weekends. About a year earlier, I had inadvertently run into this club. I came up behind a large group of people, most going at a steady pace. I had intended to go around them, but I ended up sticking with them until they ended their run. I started talking to a few of the club members and joined up.

I didn't have much social interaction outside of the Bureau. It was hard to find people that could relate to our line of work and hours. But the run club was great. Most people didn't share what they did for work and that was just fine by me. The only one who knew what I did was Justin, he was the organizer of the group. He was a cool guy and he always had great advice for improving my technique. I don't take constructive criticism very well, but his unsolicited suggestions actually helped me cut my half marathon time down by 10 minutes.

Each week we would all discuss different running gear, or training methods. Some would sign up to do fun-runs together, but most of the group was focused on The Broad Street Run and then the Philadelphia Marathon.

As I approached the run shop, there were already a few of the club members loitering around. I was welcomed heartily by Justin, our de facto leader. He was short, bearded, and always up for making others laugh. I assumed that he was a drama teacher of some kind when we first met, but because of our connection via social media, I did know that he was a graphic designer.

When the weather was beautiful, as it was that day, we usually saw an up-tick in group membership. Most of the die-hards persisted through the winter and they comprised the core group. I was one of the core-group.

Justin and his fiancé, Jasmine, were talking to a woman who had joined us for the weekly run a few times throughout the summer. She was timid, and shy, and clearly was just starting to get into shape. I rolled my eyes. *Wasn't this a group for serious runners?*

A few of the other core group members approached:

Rod, Tom, and a guy that I was fairly sure went by Tiger. I couldn't be sure, when he had first introduced himself a year earlier it really sounded like he said, "My name is Tiger." I didn't want to offend him and react in a rude way so I accepted this. And then I never felt that it was the right time to ask him his name again.

After another 10 or so minutes of chatting about the weather and hearing about the status of Rod's shin-splints, some new faces had joined the group. A few were a little familiar, others I had never seen before. This was going to be a big group, which made Justin happy. He would have a larger audience to try his latest jokes on.

We took off at 6:00 sharp. I heard the dissonant chirps of the different tracking watches beeping as the group members activated their devices. My stamina had improved since joining the club. In addition to my other weekly workouts to stay in shape for work, I was one of the out-in-front runners, keeping stride with Justin and Tom. I had even been able to start running the steps, a solid sign that I was no slow-poke.

We made it up to the third tier of steps on the Art Museum before returning to the street to join the rest of the group. It felt great to do something that my body was just good at doing. I was strong. I had always been strong and in shape, but on that afternoon, I could feel that I was really strong, healthy, and fit.

The group finished up by 6:50 pm, the leaders were already stretching and chatting as the stragglers came in. Justin had been a good leader in that he insisted on everyone meeting up again when we finished and not letting the slower folks in the club feel left out. I would have been happy to head straight to the bar instead of waiting, but everyone else waited, so I did too. Apparently Jasmine had taken the initiative to work out a deal with the bar owner so that we could enjoy some discounted appetizers each week. We were regulars and we could use this as a selling point to encourage people to join the group. The restaurant made more off us this way; it was a win-win.

We sauntered into The Happy Rooster and found our usual corner. I usually would have ordered my standard Yuengling, but the more health conscious members of the club always opted for the gluten-free option. I caved to peer-pressure (or rather beer-pressure) and went with that too. It didn't taste too bad and it made that beer special. *I only drink gluten-free beer when I'm with my running buddies.* I made a meme of myself, *I don't always drink gluten-free beer, but when I do it's because I've just run 10k.*

I spent the early part of that evening talking with Jasmine who was happy to share the details of the latest wedding plans she was working on with Justin. Justin was talking with the newer runners. I probably should have been doing that too. I had a million little excuses not to, that really added up to the fact that I just didn't want to make small-talk.

I finished my beer and enjoyed the chips and spinach dip that I had split with Rod. At an appropriate hour, I made my way to the door. I said my good-byes and "see ya next week" to the members of our group that I was standing closest to. I was heading towards the front door, which happened to be where Justin was standing. I waved good-bye, not wanting to interrupt the conversation he was having with one of the girls that was new to our group. I still don't know her name, she only showed up once or twice after that week.

As I passed Justin called out, "Hey man!"

"Good run today. See ya next week!" I waved and continued walking.

"Wait, wait," he beckoned me over. Justin was always a gregarious fellow; he was overly friendly and social even when sober. After two beers, he was everyone's best friend. "I barely got to catch up with you," he waved me over with his free hand, the nearly empty beer bottle occupying the other.

"Eh, not much to report. Felt good today, I can feel my mile-splits getting faster."

"That's great, you're gonna need that to rank in your age group next year at Broad Street."

I shrugged off the competitive dare he was making, hoping that if I seemed nonchalant that I would protect my ego if I didn't rank. I also knew I had the better part of a year ahead to improve, or injure myself. "Eh, we'll see. I want to enjoy the experience of the run. I'm not going out for a ranking."

"Yeah, ok." Justin made a face suggesting that he was onto my game. His closely trimmed beard exacerbated his expressions. You might have expected it to mask his emotion, but it seems to have grown onto him. The beard latched into his nerve endings and became an extension of his expressive gestures. At this point the new girl to our group had been pulled into a conversation with Jasmine about her running tights, they were apparently very fashionable.

"Well, you're definitely gonna rank, so you don't have to sweat it." I figured complimenting Justin would make him happy in his intoxicated state and perhaps give me the chance to leave.

"Ah man. You never know," he shrugged. "But hey, this is a big week for you. You holding up okay?"

His comment perplexed me and rendered me speechless. The first thought that ran through my mind was that he knew about Traveler. *How could he know about the case? Did he know who the Traveler was?*

Then, it hit me. It was just like the terrifying moment in a film when you see the serial killer in a flash of lightning before the theatre is engrossed in total darkness. I realized what he meant by his flippant comment: *Avila.* I furrowed my brow and pursed my lips. My shoulders were raised; my hands went into my pockets. I was in a defensive positon.

"Uh, what do you mean?" My immediate reaction was to play dumb, to pretend that my mind hadn't quickly riddled out the meaning.

"You know," Justin gestured with his hand, as though his quick motions were a foreign sign language for me to riddle out.

I shook my head. I wasn't going to say it. I was scared silent that he was about to bring her up.

"You know, your old lady," Justin rested his gesticulating hand on my shoulder. "I know that this has gotta be a tough week on you. The posters are everywhere. I want you to know, me and Jasmine, we're here for you man."

I shook my head. I knew I should have never accepted his friend request, but I didn't have many genuine friends at the time. Actually, I didn't have any genuine friends. He would have seen old photos from parties that I hadn't bothered to un-tag. He would have easily done the mental math to figure out that in another life, I was once the love interest of Avila Chase. I thought that I had been making a good connection with the run club. In that moment though, it was stained like a purloined sack of cash with a dye bomb. I'll have to quit the club. *I'll have to block Justin on Facebook. I'll have to finally un-tag those photos, and change my name, and leave the country.*

"Yeah, thanks." My social abilities shut down at the mention of her. Another flash of lightning in my mind. She, the elusive serial killer of my imagination, was now closer. She was coming for me. She was looming in the darkness ready to sink her knife into my stomach. "Uh, I really gotta get going man. I have an early day tomorrow."

"Alright, alright," Justin put his arms over his head, showing his surrender. "But you call if you need me. I got you man!" He flashed his charismatic smile and I gave a subdued smirk in return. The rational part of my brain kept telling me to keep my cool. *He was just trying to be a friend; I could use one right now.* The emotional side of my brain kept screaming to be heard, *screw you Avila, you ruin everything!*

I walked home briskly, feeling a strange paranoia. I had seen in each face that I passed, the knowing glance; I was exposed and my deepest fears had been laid bare. I heard footsteps behind me. They were almost rhythmic: *Av-ila. Av-ila. Av-ila.* The syllables of her name called out in a pattern. At least that is what they sounded like. Perhaps they could have been: *Trav-eler. Trav-eler. Trav-eler.* I tried to keep my head down, ducking eye contact, and walking faster with each step. The pattern kept repeating, but I could hear those steps getting closer and closer. The person making these sounds was right behind me.

My pace quickened as I almost broke out into a run back to my apartment. I refused to look behind me as I fumbled with the keys and let myself into the building. The person who had been so close behind me surely had no control over the sounds of their steps. My mind had planted those words there. *Av-ila. Av-ila. Av-ila.*

I had somehow mapped the posters with Avila's seeing eyes and avoided them along my route. She was an intricate bundle of gray coated wires; each alive with electric current and ready to shock you. Her eyes would only remind me of that. I ran up the stairs to my apartment, too agitated to take the calm and even-paced elevator.

I kicked off my sneakers and tried to take a few

calming deep breathes, but I felt my chest tighten and my trachea pinch with each attempt. I quickly unscrewed the top of a water bottle. I was squeezing it so tightly in my hand that water spilled out all over me. I took a heavy swig before placing the bottle down on the counter and starting the process of cleaning up my mess. The last thing I needed was to slip and fall on a small puddle in my own kitchen and give myself a concussion.

After I had cleaned up the kitchen and finished the rest of the bottle of water, I felt significantly calmer. I had already begun to chastise myself for how silly I had been.

Would I let my own ego get in the way of my mental calm? What Justin had said was the actual truth, it was a rough week for me. *Why was I so determined to deny her?* I didn't have to do it often, but telling people I didn't know her was easy now. I told that lie often enough to make Peter look like a loyal Apostle. I didn't want to just be "Avila's ex" forever, but it was the most present part of my identity. I didn't know how to distance myself from it. I began to finally ruminate of the true source of my worry. *What if she did write me in? What if it is horrible? What if it is true, and I have to face that I am no more than a common villain, an expendable character?*

I refused to turn on the television. I had tried to distract myself with it the night before without much luck. I went to bed and concentrated on the hairline cracks in the plaster ceiling above me. I tried to focus on my joints, sore and tired from the run. I went about the task of boring myself so that I could fall, and stay, asleep.

In the first dream that evening, I found myself in a living room of an unfamiliar apartment, the sounds of typing and chewing were the only things I could hear at first. This dream was so vivid, I could have sworn I had been transported in time and space to a moment in another reality. Given the all-encompassing nature of my thoughts that week, it should have been no surprise that the person I saw in this dream was Avila.

She sat alone with her computer and her thoughts. I can still picture her in that room: sitting at her desk, clacking away at the keyboard, really digging into me with her latest lines. She was blaring some pissed-chic pop or maybe it was the tantrum of a female rock-and-roller through the thin speakers of her desktop. I could see the fine details of those fiery red locks of hers, large voluminous waves moving like the tide as her head bobbed along to the beat. A paragraph finished, an indictment against me, and just in time for the hook of the song. I could see her, waving her finger at a picture of me as if to say "I told you not to mess with me."

Could she be this worked up so many years after the fact? Could this all just be in my head? I sure hoped so.

Do you have squeamish nightmares and call out to your mommy in the pitch black of our old bedroom, now yours alone? Do you watch those scary scenes in your mind of my nipples morphing into oversized and obese tardigrades, awakened and scurrying over to you, so that they feast on the skin cells that you shed unconsciously?

-Scarlett Moore and the Hopeless Case of the Poltergeist

Wednesday started after another bad night of sleep. It left a darkness just beneath my eyes that highlighted every toss, turn, and nightmare. I dressed in a full suit: black on black with a crisp white button-down and blue-knitted tie. As I made the knot in the tie, it reminded me of the vision of Avila from the night before last, the lines of text being tied into a rope. I shivered at the thought.

I dressed for my meeting with Roman, knowing that I needed to secure the necessary access to the web logs in order to file the arrest warrant for the Traveler. He was within my reach, almost too quickly.

I tried to override each thought of jealousy that I once felt toward Roman as I prepared. I began to reason with myself that even if he and Avila were together, it would actually be a blessing to me. Not only would it vindicate me, but I certainly would not want to be with her either. I tried to be the rational adult that was able to successfully investigate and conclude cases. I needed to be the professional version of myself that morning. I could afford no slip-ups as the result of my personal pains.

When clearing my mind that morning, I started to realize that, for as much as I had been focused on his role in the dissolution of my relationship with Avila, I didn't know much about Roman at all. I had only a vague mental image of this man who was the acid that etched and carved through the tenuous fibers of what had at one time been a fragile and blossoming love.

After much delay, bordering on incompetence really, I made my way to the RF headquarters in a trendy corner of the old Wannamaker building. I had evaded this interaction for months because of my personal aversion to the man. And it was during that fated week that we were finally thrust into the same time and space.

I navigated past the confused tourists funneling out of Suburban Station, the gawkers who stopped to photograph City Hall, and shouldered my way through the brass-lined revolving door and over to the elevators.

As I entered the offices of Roman's Forum, Inc. (RF), I was surprised at the efficient use of space. For what was most certainly a small square footage, the offices looked spacious. It was chock-full of genius millennials hyped on caffeine and coding. A receptionist took my name and offered me water before she picked up her phone to relay my presence.

"A Mr. Hobbertson is here to see you." Her voice was small and liquid. *Agent Hobbertson*, I corrected her in my mind. I didn't want to start out on the wrong foot. I was already more likely to slip up and say the wrong thing in front of Roman. I suddenly felt scrawny and perhaps too thin. The mental sewage of insecurity was beginning to bubble up.

During my brisk walk to the RF office that morning, I had tried to think of the Phillies current record, the potential SEPTA strike, anything and everything to keep my mind off the omnipresent topic that was devouring all of my errant thoughts. On my walk down Market Street, I focused on each piece of liter that I passed, eyeing the scraps of trash and discarded paper cups. I had actually begun to count them. The effect was very positive. I had a new resolution to volunteer for a city clean-up project and I had successfully kept Avila from my thoughts for a decent duration of time. Sitting in that waiting area though, there was very little to distract myself with. I couldn't stare at the office workers without appearing hostile or odd. I focused instead on my knuckles, but they weren't very interesting.

Finally, the receptionist, with her tightly wound and pinned back strawberry-blonde hair, called me to follow her to Mr. Trecki's office. She was the very picture of northern city women with her gray pencil skirt and black cardigan.

I remained focused on the clean cut of the receptionist's clothes and the calm patterns on the Berber carpet to keep my mind distracted as I followed her. It seemed that with each step the suppressed thoughts were creeping in.

You need to focus. *Think of the case. Keep the details fresh in your mind.* I thought about the specific request I needed to make, the impact it would have on the case, and preventing such egregious abuses and fraud from proliferating. *Yes, proliferating, use that word when Trecki asks for a reason!* I remember thinking that it would be such an excellent verb and that I would look more competent if I used it.

As the receptionist reached the door, I saw her delicate hands tap lightly on the wooden panel. Her light hair appeared darker for a moment and my mind played the cruelest of jokes on me. As she began to turn around I felt cold sweat on my neck, my heart began to race, and I braced for impact. In that fraction of a second I was positive that the receptionist had transformed into Avila. Her hair turning colors before my eyes, her skin draining of color and hue, and her teeth bared in a snarl.

But this was a neurotic trick of my psyche. She was in fact still the receptionist. I must have had the look of death on my face. She patted me on the shoulder and said, "Mr. Trecki is a nice man. Not like those other types of CEOs that you hear about. You'll do fine."

With her sensitive grace she was gone and I was left with an ajar door in front of me and a mouth as dry as the Sahara Desert.

I stepped into his office. It was small, but it had the illusion of space with a very Spartan design. There was the desk, metal and glass, with some files on top of it and a high powered laptop hooked up to multiple monitors. There were two wire-framed chairs in front of the desk and wide lanes on either side. The man behind the desk was turned away from me, looking at one of the drawers in the cabinet behind the desk. He was seated and his twisted back gave him the illusion of a hunchback, which I will admit did give me a moment to disarm the man mentally.

The morning sun was pouring into the room and gave everything a clean look, but there were still dust-mites twirling and dancing in the errant rays of light. I had pictured him sitting in a cramped basement without any windows and heaps of files towering and spilling onto the floor. I should have expected more from the man who built such a powerful company, but you have to keep in mind that first impressions lie heavy on the brain. When I first heard mention of him, at that small party years ago, I pictured a starved and flailing entrepreneur. I wasn't prepared to face his professional success, especially when it compared to his success in the case of our mutual –

"Love," I heard the sandpaper voice say.

"What?" I responded without any thought, my tone cruel and quick. *Had he just read my mind?*

"Hello?" Roman asked again. What I heard was my own version of his parapraxis, what I hoped he would say to start the conversation; the conversation that I wished would never happen. He was now facing me and he was staring at me with his eyebrows raised. His expression posing the question: *Are you okay?*

"Yes, hello," I snapped back into the reality of the moment. "Thank you for taking time to meet with me. I am Special Agent Hobbertson" I extended my arm to shake his hand.

He cautiously leaned forward and reached his hand out. He didn't even get up out of his seat, which I took as a sign of his self-perceived superiority. He was indeed handsome, and looked about the same as he had when I had looked him up on social media years before. He was tan with dark features, his forearms were visible and they were toned. Unconsciously, I covered my right forearm with my left hand.

"Roman Trecki. Glad to be of service when the nation calls. How can I help you?" Roman sat with his arms folded in front of him. He quickly reached across and pressed the small button on his monitor, shutting off the display. He was either trying to hide something, or trying to give me his undivided attention. I still can't be sure which it was.

"Yes, as I explained to your receptionist yesterday ..." I went into the long explanation about the Traveler, who I referred to as the suspect for the sake of appearing professional. I explained how he was manipulating the RF servers to hide his fraud. Roman nodded along and listened acutely. He scribbled a quick note on a small pad of paper next to his left hand. He held his pen the way a right-handed person would, but he wrote with his left. He didn't have the curved wrist movement and the dragging motion so prevalent among lefties. I was distracted by this observation as I came to the end of my explanation.

In the brief moment where my monologue lapsed, Roman interjected. "So, you want access to the logs to get the evidence to accurately pin-point this guy and prosecute him." He furrowed his brow and his arms were taught. His hairline was sharp and well defined, but his short haircut was starting to reveal the slightest hint of gray pepper through his non-descript brown hair.

"Uh, yes. That is exactly what I would like." I was pleased with his candid ability to grasp the concepts presented.

"Well, you didn't need to meet with me to do that. You could have sent a warrant over to our security team." He looked at me as though he were interrogating me. Had he been equally dreading this meeting? Had he also scanned through my social feeds with trepidation that morning?

"I prefer to work on good faith with people. No one wants their system to be the one known for criminal activity. No one wants to see their company's name dragged through the mud. I find that asking for help is often the easiest option."

Roman smiled and turned his head towards the window. He nodded his head and prepared to respond. His eyes narrowed in the direct sunlight, but he seemed to be coming to a decision of some kind. "You realize that this puts me in a precarious situation."

I was not expecting that. *Was he referring to Avila? Was he about to delay the work of a federal agency over an ex-girlfriend?*

"How so?" I wanted him to say it. I wanted him to spell it out and put it on the line. *Come on Roman, just admit that you and Avila are out to get me!*

"You know, most of the people that use RF for their website are bloggers, small businesses, and generally good people. I want to cooperate with your investigation, but I also want to be sensitive to the general climate of distrust that surrounds the federal government and its agencies."

Oh, that was a much more logical and valid reason.

"Of course," I responded and nodded my head while I was trying to formulate a response. "We don't want you to appear to be feeding your clients to the wolves, but keep in mind that the websites that are being used in this process likely have no idea that their pages are being manipulated. You are also helping those bloggers and small business owners when you help us."

He held up his hand as though to stop me.

"I want to help you Agent Hobbertson, but I thought about this yesterday. I am within my rights to refuse and request that you produce a warrant. This gives me a way to help you, but to also defer any suspicion that our policy is to just hand out information to the Feds."

I had to cut him some slack, he had thought out the request and anticipated my next moves. I reached into the breast pocket of my blazer and produced the warrant.

"I like to come prepared." I smiled congenially as I handed the document over to him. He read through the warrant and inspected the signature.

He looked up from the document and smirked. His cheeks dimpled and he let out a soft laugh. "Excellent, I will ask Tracey to show you to our system team and they can provide you with the exact information that you need."

"We would actually prefer if the data could be handed over via a portable hard drive. If we go to court, we will need to present the evidence and have it reviewed on

multiple occasions. I can't just say, 'well, I saw the logs.'"
Roman seemed to have taken that comment as a shock.

"Ah, yeah I guess that does make sense." He folded up the warrant and handed it back to me.

"I brought a clean portable drive with me as well," the thin but dense drive was in my left pants-pocket. It was powerful and compact. It always seemed weird every time I had to mention that I happened to have a 2 terabyte hard-drive in my pants. It never worked well as a joke. I really did have a hard drive in my pocket.

"Well, in this case, I may insist that you use one of our hard-drives. Otherwise you'll spend forever trying to get past the encryption." He reached around into one of the cabinets behind him. His torso was almost completely twisted around when he managed to palm the drive. He composed himself and handed it to me from across the desk.

"Great, thank you Mr. Trecki." I began to stand up. *That wasn't so bad*, I began to think to myself. But I also began to wonder if, that was it? All of my mental anguish that week and now a passive and easy interaction. Granted, Avila wasn't Roman. I couldn't blame him for her actions. But I had been so focused on her friendship with him that I had come to unilaterally associate him with our break-up.

"Call me Roman," he said kindly. "This meeting was quicker than I thought it would be, I'll save Tracey the trip and introduce you to the team myself."

I watched him as he reversed and wheeled himself

around the desk. His unusual actions now made more sense. He didn't stand to shake my hand because he couldn't. I started to feel like the real jerk: able-bodied and secretly harboring a hatred of a man who was in a wheelchair. Then I recalled one of the first things Avila ever said to me about him. "We've shared a common tragedy, that is a bond that isn't easily broken, I don't except you to understand." Perhaps the injury that cost him his mobility was related to that tragedy.

Roman must have caught my eyes as they followed the wheels on his chair. "Eh, you should see the other guy," he uttered in an inconsequential manner.

"Oh really?" I was genuinely shocked by his comment, and somewhat embarrassed to be caught looking so directly at his wheels.

"Yeah, a 30-foot flat sheet of granite." My reaction must have been enough of an invitation to elaborate. "Squirrel suit diving in Brazil earlier this year. The physical therapy is going well. I expect to be out of the chair in a month or so." Roman wheeled himself ahead of me and reversed, backing into the door of this office to push it open.

"Wow, that's pretty extreme." I was genuinely impressed, intrigued, and intimidated in equal parts.

"Yeah, I'm lucky to be alive and all that good stuff. I'm just so sick of this dang chair." Roman led me down the hallway past the reception area and to a small room. He rapped on the door and a few moments later a gawky young man appeared, wide-eyed and skittish.

"Is this a test?" he asked in a matter of fact tone.

"No Jake, this isn't a test. I can't see the entire keypad to enter the code. It's okay, you can let me in." I estimated that Roman wasn't exaggerating. The keypad for this door was at eye-level for a standing adult. He might have been able to punch in the keys if he had memorized the code, but he would have risked fat-fingering the numbers.

The young man, who Roman called Jake, looked at his boss through the thin glass in the door and then looked over to me.

"What about him?"

"He's a federal agent," Roman's scratchy voice sounded gruff and firm.

"Oh, well. Okay." The young man opened the door and allowed us both in.

"Jake, thank you," Roman said as he wheeled into the server room. "Jake, I would like you to meet Agent Hobbertson with the FBI."

"Hello." Jake nodded and waited for further information from Roman. He pushed his glasses up on the bridge of his nose. I made a small gesture to begin to extend my hand, but quickly realized that Jake was not the type to shake hands. He was already back at his chair by the time Roman and I were past the door frame. *So there was a windowless room after all*, I thought as I scanned the layout of the space.

"Jake, Agent Hobbertson has a very specific warrant for information. We value our user's privacy here, but we don't want to be played for suckers if people are using our sites to commit fraud."

"Of course," Jake responded matter-of-factly. He pushed his glasses up on his nose again, it was obviously a nervous tick. They were practically flat against the bridge of his nose.

"Let's load the data in this warrant onto one of our portable drives and then Agent Hobbertson can be on his way." Roman was instructing Jake like a school-teacher. I became mildly suspicious about what information they might be hiding, but my realm was financial crimes. I wasn't going to start digging into other matters, especially given the glaring conflict of interest that I was avoiding.

"Yes, sir," Jake reached out his hand to me, wordlessly requesting the warrant. Within a few moments all of the information I needed was loaded and ready to go.

Jake handed over the external drive, it was still warm from the recent surge of data deposited into the block. Roman thanked Jake and left him to his secure room. The entire situation had been very transactional, as though this employee had actually been a robot, or a manifestation of the computer logs in human form.

Jake appeared relieved to be left alone again. *Some people just work better with machines.* On the way back to reception Roman explained that Jake was the only employee he trusted with the server data and that he took his job very seriously.

As we reached the receptionist's desk, Roman said his farewell before wheeling himself back to his office. "Tracey can assist you with anything else that you need.

Hopefully you will be able to close your case now."

"Yes, thank you." I was left standing with the harddrive. Diligent Tracey was sitting behind her desk, paying attention to the interaction with great detail.

I stood there for a silent moment, trying to make sense of the miss-matched emotions in my head. *He was congenial and polite. But he must know who I am. Perhaps he doesn't care who Avila was with after they broke up. Perhaps he hasn't kept up with her at all. Or maybe, they are still together and they will have a laugh at my expense later this evening.* I couldn't help but think how cruel Avila was.

"Is there anything else I can help you with Mr. Hobbertson?" Tracey asked. She was either ignorant of the proper address being 'Agent' or she was intentionally trying to get under my skin.

I was about to say, "no, I'm good" and walk out when I had a wicked little thought. *I wonder what he is doing on Friday?*

"Yes, actually. We usually can wrap up these technology-related cases pretty quickly. I'd like to be able to stop by and thank Mr. Trecki for his help once we've made our arrest. Is he busy this Friday?"

"He is in meetings all morning and then he is leaving early for an event." Tracey didn't even need to glance at the screen. She had his schedule memorized.

"Oh well. I'll have to make a note to stop by on Monday then." I smiled, but I could sense that Tracey wasn't fooled by my farce. She returned a smile, but I could see that she was being polite by the ways her eyes narrowed and evaluated me.

"Have a nice day Mr. Hobbertson." She emphasized the *'Mister'* with extra care.

"Thank you," I walked away before I could return a verbal barb and make myself look even more like a fool.

The interaction with Roman had been easier than planned. I handed off the hard-drive to our team that specialized in scrubbing data and securing it for evidence. All I had to do was wait for the final confirmation and file the request for the arrest warrant. The Traveler was in my sights.

I filled in Director Knight, but left out the internal mental dialog I had throughout the meeting with Roman Trecki. Knight seemed pleased by my recounting of Roman's concerns over privacy and his insistence on a search warrant.

"What did I tell you? Always have the warrant as a back-up." He gestured with his index finger as though he was pointing to that exact memory on an invisible string in his office.

"You sure did," I nodded and let the man enjoy his moment to recount and retell the same lessons he had already verbalized. Knight was a man of nostalgia, he thrived on retelling the same anecdotes and stories over and over. I could tell that he rehearsed the timing and the pauses. No doubt, this moment would end up becoming a lesson that he would verbally share with new agents. He would likely add on a few embellishments, no doubt.

I was too anxious to eat as I waited for the final notification from the data team. I paced by the desk and then started to meticulously organize my files. I had a few bad guys to look into, but my focus was zeroed-in on the man who had almost enough money to make a clean getaway. I had closed-in on the Traveler so easily. Maybe the Traveler was trying to become incarcerated so that he could live off of the system permanently. Perhaps he was really looking to make off with a lifetime of free meals, cable TV, and endless free time to read. Stranger things had been recorded in FBI history.

Finally, at 2pm I heard the muted ping that indicated a new e-mail had come into my Outlook inbox. I checked the results and sure enough, Traveler was working out of a house in Seattle. I met with Knight immediately to coordinate an arrest with the Seattle field office. I filed the papers for an arrest warrant. I made extremely detailed notes that would be sent over to my counterpart on the west coast.

I did finally grab a sandwich as I waited for a response from the team in Seattle. We held a conference call at the end of the day and had everything coordinated for a quick arrest. Both Knight and I stressed the urgency of the matter and the potential flight-risk of the suspect given the amount of money that he had pilfered.

Knight concluded the call and asked that we be kept up-to-date on the operation. The plan was for an early morning raid the following day. Early morning for the Seattle team meant normal time for us on the east coast.

We had a plan in place. I told Knight I would be in much earlier than usual to be able to handle any last minute issues, should they come up.

It was well past 8pm when I left the office. I was excited to know that we were so close to catching the Traveler, but I felt the usual wave of worry knowing that there would be a few more hours where this man was free to steal again, and free to run.

I made my way home along the dark streets of my city. I found a calm in the sounds of my footsteps along the pavement, just mine alone. I took a longer route home and passed by Independence Mall, empty except for a few errant tourists snapping photos. The bell tower was lit impeccably and the visitor center was quiet. As the others left the park, I could have fooled myself for a moment that I wasn't in a modern century. In the darkness, Philadelphia always looks so revolutionary.

The evening was cool. Fall was well on its way and there was no amount of wishing or longing for summer that could stop it. I found my mind wandering to the long walks I had taken through the city. Usually I was going somewhere, always aiming for a specific destination. That night I recalled the most aimless of my walks, the one that served as my purgatory and my punishment.

I still can't even remember exactly how that argument began, all those years ago. It must have been like the others. In my memory, I had reviewed it so many times and tried to make sense of the order of who threw what words at each other and when, that I must have rearranged them at some point. I knew that I had been growing more and more jealous of the time Avila was spending without me. I was suspicious of her time with friends, *was she really with friends or was she with Roman?* She had called me out on my attempts to control who she was seeing and what she was doing with her time. I accused her of cheating. She accused me of being paranoid.

In that moment I was so overwhelmed with contempt, I felt that Avila's words had started to attack me.

So, I lost control.

I snapped and I hit her square in the jaw. Not with an open-palmed slap, but with a clenched fist. Avila absorbed the full force of it and stared at me, shocked and scared. Her skin instantly flashed red and her eyes began to well with tears. Pain consumed her expression.

I left right then, without a word. I wandered the city aimlessly throughout that night. Once dawn broke I found a diner. I stayed until that afternoon when I found a bar. I didn't return to the scene of that last interaction, the scene of my crime, until it was evening again. As I expected, and hoped, she was gone.

That's right, I just left. I'm the bad guy all along.

At least I was. I'm not a bad guy now and I would never- I guess it doesn't matter what I say now. I'm condemned, by myself, by her, by you. Worst of all, her punishment will be slow, drawn out, and incredibly detailed.

That's it. That is the root of the fear that was

consuming me. I was waiting for her worst, her detailed and piercing cross-examination of my personality, my flaws, and my motives for being the guy that hit her.

That is the reason why I was the perfect specimen for a revenge novel, I am the villain in her story. After all, the novel was titled *Scarlett: Avenged*. It had to be my turn, it just had to be.

When I had reached my apartment, I sat pensively on my couch, hunched over and finally being honest with myself.

I knew that soon, once the book was released, the written character that was supposed to represent me would be hated by many. They will shake their heads as they read the details of my appearance, my walk, my swagger. The words would bleed before my eyes and stain my hands like red stamp ink as I read the passage that detailed what I did that evening: the violence and the cowardice.

I never spoke to her again after that night. I knew that anything I could say would just sound cliché and would feel false on my tongue. I stayed silent. Might she have noticed that it was a penitent silence? Would Avila forgive my moment of rage and recognize the many good moments that we had before that horrible night?

I had stopped drinking for a time after our relationship ended. I was convinced that my fit of rage must have been sourced from a well of fire in my stomach. I stopped going out to the bars where the music was loud and the lights were low. I could feel her presence there, following me, reverberating from the deep bass line. I spent a long time denying myself any entertainment or fun, until, little by little, I broke back into my normal routines.

The words from the *Philadelphia Magazine* interview rang fresh in my mind, emblazoned and empowered.

*"Scarlett may be investigating paranormal activities, but it is always human errors that bring her back into this world. **I wanted to focus on an issue that is important not just to women, but to society. We can't just say this is a woman's issue anymore, it's a human issue.** Through Scarlett I can bring this problem to the forefront of our consciousness and hopefully spur change."*

There could be no mistaking her words. My time was up. Avila was ready to disclose her true hatred for me and avenge herself through Scarlett.

I closed my eyes that night as I tried to fall asleep. All that I could see where those piercing green eyes from the poster. They were staring at me. Like Fitzgerald's oculist, her eyes could see all, silently passing judgment.

After another night of little to no sleep, that Thursday morning came unwanted and unwelcomed. I had set an alarm to get up earlier than usual and each inch of my body resisted the blaring sound, urging me to get up, to move, and to get to work.

I purchased two large coffees on the way into the office and found that Director Knight was in his office, scanning through some documents. He thanked me for the coffee and we both headed to our conference room to wait for verbal and visual confirmation of the raid and arrest. This would be yet another small success on my pile of "always trying to prove to myself that I am a successful person."

As I continue to tell you the events of that week, the pre-amble to a significant turning point in my life, know that even further back into my past was a tumultuous and rolling relationship with Avila. We had glorious moments of happiness and affection. But within her was an independence. Something forcefully uncontrollable that couldn't be restrained. She saw no issue on the topic of staying in contact with her ex, Roman, and no ability to see the mistrust from my point of view. Within me, contempt started to brew, bubble, and ferment. I couldn't get her to see my side and now everyone in the world would only know her side. It felt so unfair, I felt so jilted by my impending punishment. But, with each successful case closed, I began to feel more self-affirmed. I began to feel the confidence that had once defined me, begin to breathe life back into me. That morning was about so much more than another arrest; it was about proving that I was still right.

I was unfocused and exhausted that morning. I should have been alert. I should have been thinking through all of the possible methods for the raid to go wrong. But I was distracted by the looming deadline for *Scarlett: Avenged* to be released.

I brought my laptop into the conference room to check through emails as the video feed was being set up. I clicked through some smaller items that didn't require my attention and then sorted them away. I saw a few red flags pop-up for new fraud activity. It appeared as though several new bad guys were popping up and all using the same method of hacking into gift cards, but they were all using new websites that I hadn't encountered before. After a quick glance, I could see that none of them ran through the RF server.

My cognitive gears were firing on a delay; however, my synapses were finally starting to wake up. I checked the usual routes of the Traveler. It appeared that he had tried to make another large deposit in the late evening hours, but was blocked. I began to come to the realization, RF *would have closed the potential loophole as soon as I left so as to keep this kind of activity from persisting.*

That would have tipped off the Traveler for sure. The new flags that I registered in the early hours of that Thursday morning could have been new activity, or it could have been this same exact guy trying to finish off his scheme before leaving.

Director Knight was sipping on his coffee and eyeing the video screen, peering above the rim of his glasses. The agents were starting to take their places flanking each other outside of the apartment. "We should check to see if this guy has made any travel plans." I was trying to hide the panic in my voice.

"What?" Director Knight muttered, his attention fully

focused on the video screen.

"I think he may have already left, we should call these agents back." I tried to keep my voice level to mask how problematic the situation was.

"Huh?" Knight finally looked over at me, just as the agents on the video screen were using a battering-ram to break down the suspect's apartment door.

"I think he split early, he won't be there." I turned my attention to the screen. The chaos of watching a half-dozen agents burst into an apartment from the viewpoint of a thin camera was jarring. The constantly moving picture left me nauseated as we waited for some kind of signal that the suspect was captured. What we heard instead was that the apartment was empty.

"No one here," a voice managed to squeeze through the radio static. "Place is empty, must have been tipped off."

Indeed, the Traveler had been tipped off and was on his way. When his usual path had been blocked through Roman's Forum he found an alternative route, transferred the money quickly, and took off. While this was in the criminal's nature to evade us, I was supposed to keep us one step ahead.

As the agents began to set about the work of cataloging the items remaining in the apartment, a loud pop came through the thin speakers in the conference room and the video screen went blank. After frantic calls we confirmed that a small explosive device did go off in the apartment. While it wasn't big enough to cause structural damage, several agents were severely burned. Those moments, those hours, passed around me like water. They felt like a numbing cold stream crossing over me, burying me, drowning me beneath its weight.

All of my small successes paled in comparison to this glaring error in judgment. It was the item I had neglected, and my preoccupation with Avila was to blame. Director Knight had signed off of the conference call, I was too shamed to speak. For a mild mannered man, he sure could berate an employee.

If my head was hanging low that morning after the muffed arrest and explosion, it continued to droop and sag throughout the day. I had to file paperwork, answer to Director Knight's boss, hear the chatter in the breakroom stop abruptly as I walked in, and try to track the Traveler through airline an and bus records. I confirmed that the injured agents were released from the hospital and that they would return to desk-duty quickly. My only small grace was that they were not more severely injured.

The one shining ray of hope in that week of torture, my career, was considerably dimmer that afternoon.

I was in need of solace, but I had been single for months. I regretted intentionally misplacing the phone number of my Sunday evening rendezvous, wishing for some kind of human interaction to distract me. I stood outside of the office, bracing my neck against the chilly wind by folding up the collar on my jacket. After thumbing through my phone, I realized that I had never responded to Nick's texts earlier in the week. I opened up the conversation and typed a short response:

"Yeah, I'm alright. You? Drinks?"

I wasn't about to pour out my frustrations in a text message and I was loath to express them verbally as well. I wondered if the catharsis of drinking with an old friend would coax my emotions from their caged den within my mind. Perhaps if I released all of those demons I would exorcise of them for good.

I began walking aimlessly up Market Street. Every few blocks I would look back at City Hall, illuminated and omnipresent. I didn't go a day without passing it and I never tired of it. I stood admiring the structure and felt my phone buzz in my pocket.

"Yeah man. About to catch a train home, but I can stay for another hour to catch up."

Nick usually took the train through 30th Street Station each morning and evening on his way out to the suburbs. He and Claudette had moved out to Upper Dublin at some point in the previous year and now he was a regular commuter. I made a note to give him grief for living in what had so lovingly been nicknamed "Upper Dumpster."

"Not far from 30th Street myself. Sláinte?"

I started to make my way further up Market Street without waiting for Nick's response. I felt my phone buzz with his response "Here" as I was crossing the street to enter the bar.

It was unfortunately a packed house. University professors and young professionals gathered for a weekly round of some quiz game that had become somewhat boisterous. Nick and I took our seats at the far end of the bar. I thought of ordering a gluten-free beer, but decided to dive in fully and drown my tormented sorrows in whiskey and Coke.

"Hitting the hard stuff early man?" Nick inquired after I placed my order, definitely a harder drink compared to the orange-and-lime beer that he had ordered.

"Us unmarried guys get to do that every once in a while," I gave him a sly smile that invited him to tell me about his life with Claudette. They were happy with their new house. He was doing some projects to get the house into better shape, which helped to build on his limited skills.

In short order, the conversation turned to focus on what was new in my life. Usually I would answer these kinds of questions with vague updates about how much I loved me job. I didn't have much going on in my life outside of work; I had been so solitary and standoffish that my personal life was like a sinkhole, ever-empty and dangerous to approach. Since I had a bad day at work I didn't necessarily want to boast about how well I was doing. I knew that one botched mission was unlikely to result in my dismissal, but I was fairly glum about my prospects that evening.

"Not much actually, not much at all," I took a hard and open swallow of my drink.

"Yeah," Nick offered sympathetically. It wasn't as

though he was aware of how bleak my social outlook was, but he had to know that it wasn't good. "I'm sure this week doesn't make it any easier for you."

I wanted to defend myself and spurn his insights, but hadn't this been the reason that I had reached out to him? "Ah, yep. It's been tougher this time around." I nodded in agreement but couldn't make eye contact with him.

"Well, especially after we all thought that she was done writing for good." I could see him shrug in my peripheral vision. I wanted to nod along, but this was news to me. *She can't give up writing, it's her passion*, I thought instinctively. Even though her retirement would have saved me from that week of hell, it would have meant that the cat-and-mouse game that she was playing with my mind would officially be over.

And then I realized, as the whiskey began to soak into my stomach and loosen up my thoughts, that I hadn't thought much about what Avila was doing. I was focused on what I had done. I was fixated on that moment when I saw the betrayal in her eyes and had been bracing for retribution. I had spent all of that time focused on single-state Avila. The Avila who was scorned and angry, the monster of my dreams. But I hadn't taken much time to think of the giddy and excited Avila who just found out her book would become a movie, or the consciously humble Avila who was making great efforts to be gracious, or the exhausted Avila who struggled with the pressures of quick success. I had discarded all of those other versions and ignored any other possible emotion to maintain my villainous version of the person that she was.

"Uh, was she done?" I asked quietly, hoping my words would be small enough to be missed and the truth avoided.

"Yeah, yeah. She lived abroad for a year and didn't write a single word except for a few postcards home. Claudette was worried that she would have to fly over to whatever small little village she was in and shake her out of her funk, but it seems that time away actually brought her to this - " Nick paused, searching and scanning his memory for an exact word as though it were a tactile object he could pick out from the menu of beers hanging above the bar. "- Higher plane of her career." He finished his thought and took the last swig of his beer.

"Oh, wow," my voice did not echo the enthusiasm of my word choice.

"I know you probably don't want to talk about it much. It's okay. I'm here if you ever want to catch up man, but I think I need to run if I'm going to catch my train." Here was the opportunity to openly discuss the one topic that was voraciously eating into my grey-matter and Nick was leaving.

"Yeah, of course," I offered without much thought, filling the sound space with my words. "Will you be at the uh, thing tomorrow night?"

"No," he shook his head and waved his hand to display how emphatically he didn't want to go. "It's gonna be a little stuffy and we'll see Avila when she is around this weekend." His delicate manner of side-stepping her name and circumventing her had been replaced by the casual indifference of a person whose mind was focused elsewhere. He was thinking about catching his train, I was focused on catching the woman who was about to ruin my life.

"Do you know for sure if I have a reason to worry tomorrow?" I looked at my shoes. My raw and unhidden, unabashed misery was apparent in the sag of my shoulders, the stoop of my neck, and the trembling of my hands that were shoved into my pockets.

"Hey man," he beckoned me to look up. "You gotta stop worrying about this. If she did, she did. If she didn't, she didn't. I really think you aren't giving her enough credit." I could see his patience had sublimated and was now being sucked into the air vents and whisked away on the wind. He looked at me with pity.

It had been to Claudette's that Avila had fled that evening, with a loose story about tripping clumsily as she was trying to pack her things and leave. The bruise would have been obvious though. Claudette hated me from that moment on. Nick had given me the benefit of his doubt, but my behavior and worry must have exposed me by now. The look in Nick's eyes was shouting, *she could have sued you, she could have had you arrested, so maybe be quiet and take this like a man.* All of those things would have been true; perhaps I should have been more grateful for the career that I had been able to keep. But I despised the idea of being indebted to her, to that act. I didn't want to be captive for committing one crime for the rest of my life.

When I think back on that lonely evening of drinks with Nick, I realize how captive I was to my victimhood. I was so indignant in my right to be the one who was belittled and abused in that scenario. *What right did she have to use her experience in our relationship, of which I owed a 50% stake, in her creative works?* In the months that followed those fateful twenty-four hours, I have realized that I had no right to feel any ownership over her thoughts and feelings. If only I would have realized that years earlier, I might have saved myself heartache and Avila a black eye.

This hindsight is so startlingly clear, but that evening was so dark that I can only remember the stark shining street lights, the brown glow of the buildings and sidewalks, and the pitch black sky reflected on a city full of glass windows. At first I had walked quickly, my steps echoing the anger inside of me. With each firm clap of my feet on the cement I felt the satisfaction of the sound until I found myself intentionally stomping with each step to create a louder and louder sound. I would not be quiet, I would be cantankerous and impossible to avoid.

Without really trying to, I was walking by the book store. Closed and dark, the street reflected clearly on the slick glass of the storefront. I could see a stark reflection of my outline, with the empty park and the nearby lights. Behind the glass, separating me from the instrument of my insanity were the posters of Avila's staring eyes and an artfully stacked pile of her book, *Scarlett: Avenged*. A thousand pairs of her eyes glared at me, like a giant arachnid with its prey ensnared. I was looking back into my doom.

I pondered my predicament for a while on that street. No one else was around, which was eerie and peculiar. I began to think of what last desperate acts I could make to stop the next day from coming. I could find a brick, a stray rock, or a heavy trashcan and throw it into the glass. I would shatter that clean and smooth poster and send the books tumbling. I could criminally maneuver a way into the back of the store and steal the volumes of the freshly printed novel and squirrel them away so that no one could ever read the words in my hoard. I could pile each of those books in the center of the store and strike a match to watch her words burn.

I went so far as to think of pulling a different book from the shelves. Perhaps one that had an inflammatory message, so as to avoid suspicion. If a crazed religious nut broke into the bookstore and burned every version of the latest romance novel or some magic-based series for children, and Avila's book just happened to be burned up in the process, I would distance myself from suspicion. I envisioned the investigation that would follow and that the inspector would not be focused on those with a known aversion to Avila.

The plans unfolded in my head so easily, I could easily explain my alibi and make it home quickly to get a verified location at the time of the crime. I knew the master code to disarm several alarm systems. I figured that there would be a janitor's closet or a storage room with some kind of combustible chemicals to spray over the books. I was skint on matches, but made a mental note to check for some in the drawers behind the cash register.

I would have gone through with it all too, if it hadn't become abundantly obvious that I wouldn't be able to destroy every copy in the city, let alone every copy in the state or country. The book would likely be available online as well; it would find its way into millions of homes on illuminated screens. I wanted to rip out the pages that would reference the fictionalized character that Avila had written to represent me. I wanted to read it now and brace for the impact. I was so certain that she would have used this opportunity to rat me out and write me in. My hands clenched into fists reflexively as my mind spun around this new idea. I began to look around me for something to throw at the window.

To my left and right the sidewalk was clear except for imperceptible pebbles trapped in the cracks between the sidewalk blocks. No large chunk of cement broken off, no slate rock to throw. No stray bricks from the road were popping up. The closest trash can did appear to be bolted to the ground, so I knew that would be a non-starter.

The lack of resources exasperated me and validated that this evil plan should not be carried out. I stuck my fists into my jacket pocket and turned to walk home. It was a day of ruined plans.

I turned the corner and kept my head down against the wind blowing between the buildings. I passed the alley that was lined with dumpsters, where the back door to the bookstore would have been. I passed the additional posters advertising the event and continued past other closed store fronts. I was almost to the end of the block, with a clear right-of-way to continue walking, when I almost tripped on it.

I was so eager to cross the street in time to make the light, that I missed the rounded and bulbous rock. It was sitting precariously in the middle of the sidewalk and appeared to have been carefully placed there. How could it have made its way onto that exact street and into that position otherwise?

I could have picked it up, ran back to the store, and hurled the object in a matter of seconds. It appeared to me as a gift from the universe, a chance to stop the clock on my deadline with perpetual embarrassment and shame. I pictured my arm arching back and chucking the rock. I could almost hear the last shards of glass tinkling as they rained down on each other. My arm muscles began to twitch, as though anticipating the force about to be exerted. But I couldn't move. I was frozen between indecision and uncharacteristic action. Would my arm throw another blow to Avila, this time bruising and scaring her professional face? Would I find the strength to just walk away and move on?

After another moment, I heard footsteps behind me, another late-night pedestrian out on the streets. I realized that my firm stance on the sidewalk would appear unusual at best. I began walking, being forced to move along before deciding. Fate interceded to save me from criminal activity that evening. I found my way home and poured myself another glass of whiskey before slipping into an amber colored sleep.

I spent that night in a vivid dream. The streets of my city, my beloved Philadelphia, were laid out like the pages of a book. As I crossed each intersection, the pages would flip, revealing the new text that was to be offered. But as these thoughts became words, they turned out to be one word in repetition: "Avila." The pages were covered in a steady stream of her name over and over again. "Avila Avila Avila Avila Avila Avila Avila Avila," the words ran across in printed type. They were the ticker-tape of my thoughts from that past week. More accurately, they were my thoughts over the past years. I was obsessed, it was plain as day when it was all written out. Paper clouds formed above my head and began to let out the smallest little raindrops comprised of scraps of paper. In the paper-motion film-like dream, I continued to walk until finally I reached out my hand and grabbed one of the raindrops. I unfolded it and written within was, of course, "Avila." This mania was ever so transparent now.

This dream lingered with me even as I settled into my desk at work and scanned for the latest flags. The search was taking longer to run that morning so I got my coffee and avoided making eye contact with Director Knight as we crossed paths in the hallway. He didn't make an attempt to say hello. Perhaps he was avoiding me as well.

When I returned to my desk and unlocked my screen

it appeared as though an outbreak of measles or smallpox had invaded my system. Bright red flags littered my results screen, hundreds of entries deep instead of the usual dozen or so that were usually marked each morning. I checked my filters thinking that I must have made an error in the search parameters. But this was in fact the activity over the course of one day. It appeared to be an over-night explosion in gift-card fraud. I followed through on the flags and found that overnight there had been a dozen new sites started on the RF server that were created for the sole purpose of laundering the stolen gift card values.

It would appear that until additional measures were put into place I would have to be in continual contact with Roman to request log files and that these sites be shut down. I made a note of the new sites that were started and made a point to log the new sites as they appeared to look for any larger patterns that would aid in catching the persons responsible. A chilling thought caught me, *what if it was only one person responsible? What if one person was developing these sites so that other thieves could steal their funds $500 at a time?*

As I sorted through the data, the hours of the day ticked by. I was thankful for the close of business and that I had spent the day avoiding the looming event that would be held only a few blocks from my apartment, and would intersect my route home. I can admit that Avila filled my thoughts in the empty moments of that day. *Was she somewhere hidden among the code, the binary 0s and 1s of the newly discovered treasure trove of fraud? Was this her true torture?*

On my way out of the office that day I stopped to discuss the new data with Director Knight. He mulled over the information as he nodded his head. I expressed my concern over the sudden spike in activity and told him I would leave it alone over the weekend to see what patterns emerged. I planned to pay Roman Trecki and his team a visit on Monday morning if there needed to be additional measures put in place to stop the proliferation of the dummy sites.

Director Knight seemed pleased with my assessment and made a side comment about going too hard on me the day before. I told him that I had made an error and expected no less than to be called out on it. He offered to take me out for a drink, but I demurred, stating that I had plans. It tasted like a prevarication on my tongue and sodium saturated taste-buds. I didn't have plans to meet anyone or to do anything particularly. But I knew that I needed to keep my evening clear. I didn't want to mark the passing of that night with just a happenstance happy hour and a quiet evening of watching the news and reading before bed. I needed to feed my anxiety and confront my demon face-to-face: blazing green eyes and all.

They'll make a netting to ensnare you, to trap you, to catch you in the act. My medusa strands will turn you to stone as they cover and suffocate you.
-Scarlett Moore and the Golden Pegasus

I pondered my predicament on my stroll towards the bookstore. The evening was still young so I popped into a nearby restaurant for a bite to eat. *Would Avila be dining there with her friends and manager before the event? Would Roman be taking her out for a romantic dinner to celebrate the release?* I was dying to be the one to ruin her perfect evening.

The words that Nick had sent to me were streaming constantly through my mind. What perfectly curled and formed letters would be awaiting me if I ever chose to open that book? *Would a gnarled hand reach out to suffocate me? Would those words brush me off in a cavalier manner?* My thoughts were wild. And finally, just as my food arrived, steaming and greasy, I went to the dark place in my own head.

Am I really as bad as Ike Turner or Ray Rice or any of the men who share my crime?

Yes. I know the answer; the answer was and still is "Yes". I may hope for mercy, but I still know the answer. No reasoning or pages of explanation can excuse me and now I live as a man who shouldn't deserve trust. Even though I know I shouldn't have done it and have sworn to never do it again, I still don't find myself deserving of trust.

Perhaps, I wondered, *if Avila writes me out as the monster that I was that evening, I can start to forgive myself.* I had spent a momentous amount of effort fighting myself, hoping that she wouldn't expose my sins in printed word, but I was also hoping for the release. I wanted permission to own up to my evil nature and face her honest appraisals.

Would my crucible of redemption burn at the speed of light? The speed of sound? The speed of literature?

The grease had sopped into the bun of my cheeseburger and left if wilting in my hand, the slimy lettuce sliding out as my hands clamped down. My appetite had fled at the thoughts of my internal self-loathing, but I didn't dare to enter the bookstore. Not yet. I didn't want to be one of the first people there, obviously loitering and anxious to catch a glimpse of her.

As I cleared my plate and drowned my fries in ketchup, I began to envision the moment when she might see me. Would it be a smile, glad to see my after so many years? Would she duck her eyes quickly, recognizing me instantly and hoping to avoid an interaction? Would she pass over me quickly, only to realize in a nightmare that evening that I had been so close to her yet again? Or, would she grimace, delighted to see that I had shown up to face my executioner? So much would be revealed in that first interaction. I felt myself anticipating that look, much like I did when I had prepared for our initial dates. I had been anxious to impress her and read her expression.

I paid for my meal and tipped the waitress an extra smile. My hands were trembling so I shoved them into my pockets, but it did nothing to stop the jittering. If anything, the motion was exacerbated by the friction of the cloth, so I withdrew my hands and crossed them behind my back. The sun had set behind the tall buildings and marbled facades. The lights that lined the perimeter of the park, steeped in history and wonder for many a Philadelphian, were lit. I sauntered over and leaned on one of the light-poles, trying to channel the practiced cool of a Humphrey Bogart. It was a failed effort.

I let the moment hang before me. It was so weighty that I could almost see it press down on the leaves of the trees and cause the traffic signs to bend. In my veins I could feel each blood cell as it whizzed by on its way to oxygenate my limbs; I could feel the enzymes as they bounced against the plasma, I could feel each element as it was held in suspended wonder against the force of Bohr's nucleus. I could feel that it was all about to end, my torture would soon be over. I would wake up the next morning as a man free from Avila's grasp.

Finally, when I felt my hands settle and I mustered the courage, I crossed the street to enter the bookshop. The front of the store was already packed with fans eager to get their hands on a copy of Scarlett: Avenged. They were of the mindset that if they had the book before anyone else that they would be counted among the true and worthy fans of Scarlett Moore. I squeezed my way past the hoards and found an empty alleyway formed by two bookshelves. They appeared to have been pushed closer together for the event, so as to make room in the main area of the bookstore. But they were still far enough apart for me to slip through, like a secret channel leading to Avila.

As I breached the opening between the two bookshelves I saw another large group. This one was sitting quietly, and listening to a tall woman with features so simultaneously dark against skin so pale I couldn't place her nationality. She was wearing a long flowing skirt with a patterned design and a black sweater. Her thick black hair reminded me of a movie star, it appeared to be glamorous and somewhat out of place on a woman who was dressed in a new-age manner. As she spoke, she pointed to a photo of small children. These children were clearly identifiable as slum-children. Their clothes were tattered and either too big or too small. Their smiles were eager and hopeful. It was the kind of image I had seen before, but had passed mindlessly. As the woman spoke she continued to tell a personal story of the child on the right, a young girl who was doomed to a life in a brothel. This woman, unknown to me, was so captivating that I almost forgot why I was there. I became so entranced in what she was saying that I couldn't blink, I didn't dare move, until I saw *her*.

Sitting in the front row of this grouping of people, I saw the bright glitter of her vibrant hair.

It was almost like a dream coming to life. I could see the ghost of her as I passed by the bookshelves, her apparition always just around the corner. I longed to catch up, but I knew a set of fangs would greet me if I did.

After the woman's speech ended, a man stood up to applaud her and thank her for the information provided. I knew who this man was, though I had never met him in person before. It was Avila's literary agent. He was tall and thin, his graying hair only visible in a small tuft on the crown of his head. He was clearly uncomfortable with the new norms in men's fashion as he was sporting a mismatched outfit that screamed, *"I'm trying to be aloof and I hope you've noticed!"*

He informed the crowd that they would break for a few moments and then Avila would be speaking on the book and reading an excerpt to the crowd. At this she rose and waved to the crowd. Her eyes were kept at the level of those in their seats, she didn't even glance past the bookshelves in the back of the store where I was still lurking. Surely, I thought, if she had spotted me she would have given some sign. Even if she anticipated my arrival, she wouldn't be able to hide a twitch or a micro-expression on her face.

She may not have noticed me, but I was making a quick study of her. She was much more polished than I had remembered. As a younger woman she was more loose and awkward, never so tall and self-assured. Her shoulders were arched back where there used to be a timid slouch. Her clothes were well tailored and suited her body, nothing like the tight jeans and lumpy sweatshirts that she used to hide herself in. And her hair. Her bright red hair was more vibrant that I had ever pictured in my nightmares. It was so red that it was almost orange. As she subtly moved her head, smiling at another section of the crowd, it moved. Each minute, movement looked like flashes of fire dancing around her, like a halo of destruction. She had made these subtle movements so quickly and was now excusing herself, moving out of the area to avoid being waylaid by a fan or a reporter.

I moved my eyes around quickly to see if anyone would follow her. Not the reporter that was sitting in the second row, identifiable from his profile picture in the Philadelphia Magazine article. Short and wavy dirty blond hair, ruddy cheeks, and thin silver glasses were enough to be able to tell it was him. The steno pad in hand also helped. The agent had made his way over to the reporter, likely discussing some details.

I also spotted Roman, still in his wheelchair, but clearly very well dressed. He was trying to catch the attention of the woman that had been speaking. He seemed eager and nervous. Perhaps has was vying for a chance to re-enter Avila's life. *Not so close anymore, are you?* I wondered.

This was my chance. I wanted to act quickly, but I moved slowly, carefully. I was like a crouching cat of prey, moving with the balls of my feet first. I headed around the perimeter of the open seating area and noticed that she had slipped down a hallway. There were three doors: "Mens", "Ladies", "Storage." I didn't see her in the hall and didn't want her agent or anyone to see me just standing around waiting for her. In my hasty planning, I just acted and opened up the door marked storage and waited inside. I could easily back away if someone else came by, and they would shut the door, and not notice me lurking. But, if Avila came by, I could still see and take my chance to talk to her. It seemed like a half decent idea in the fraction of a second it took me to think of it.

I should have expected her to be startled. I hadn't really thought through how it must look to her. At first a voice calling to her from the shadows, then me, her ex, stepping out, surprising her. Did I scare her? Did I make her mentally check the exits and calculate whether she should scream or run? Did I have any effect on her at all?

"Oh, hi," Avila said as her eyes were widening and her breaths becoming more shallow. I had forgotten how soft her voice was, how silent she could be when she wasn't projecting to a crowd. For some reason that tiny voice hadn't remained in my memory.

"Hi," was all that I could muster. I had pictured in my mind so many times what I would say to her if we ever came face to face again. But all I could get out was the basic, "Hi."

"Oh, Trevor! Hi!" she pretended to recognize me, I figured this for a ruse. *How could she not recognize me?* What a faker, I knew she must have been faking. "How are you?"

"Uh, okay I guess," the contempt in my voice was uncontrollable. I couldn't hide how annoyed I was at her mental exercises, tricking me and tormenting me. It flooded me all at once and with the tidal wave it caused, it washed away any sentimental outcroppings that might have been budding within me.

Avila, with her long pale legs and tan heels, her overall muted and demure color scheme, didn't fool me. She looked as though she was searching for what to say next, she looked uncomfortable and ready-to-run at the first chance.

"Um, are you here to see Roman again?" she nodded her head towards the party to indicate that Roman was there. *So he did tell you about our meeting.* This immediately renewed my suspicions that they were in fact back together as a couple.

"No," I shook my head as I jutted my jaw forward. "But, I think that we need to talk." I gestured for her to follow me into the store room. After a moment's hesitation she did follow. Oh memory, please remind me of how that bright and illuminated hallway could have been the final and anti-climactic chapter in my saga with Avila. But no, it was that dank and dark store room where our story finally came to an end, our journey completed.

Once we were both inside of the store room, I grasped for the light switch, finally taking a wide swing and finding the delicate chain. I gave it a yank and the dark space was sparkly illuminated by a bald bulb swinging from the ceiling. There were stacks of boxes as far as I could see, built into shapes to give the room depth and texture.

"So, what's up?" Avila asked. There was a tone in her voice that hinted at, *"I need to get back out there, make it quick."* I turned to face her. The space that was illuminated was small, I could either stand in the shadows to speak to her, or she could stand in the shadows, or we could both stand very close to one another in the light. We naturally struck a middle-distance, both barely visible to one another on the periphery of the illumination.

"I've spent a lot of time this week thinking about you, and the book," I let my words trail off. I was starting to sound like a deranged fan. Why hadn't I thought more about what to say? "And, I thought about your old habits of writing your exes into your novels."

I heard her let out a deep sigh. She didn't start to reply, which emboldened my suspicions. Instead she made it clear that her exhausted release of air was not an admission of guilt, but of a pained and repeated defense that she had made so many times.

"I considered writing a book with you as a main character. I started the manuscript. But it was rubbish, it wasn't my style or my genre. It felt all wrong."

"What genre, romance?" I made a point to put that little wolfish smile on my face, the one she used to always say made her melt. It was my secret weapon to wiggle back into her heart.

"No, true-crime." She responded plainly, unblinking with her cavalier answer.

"Well, I know what you've been up to. Haven't you made me suffer enough?"

"Suffer? What are you talking about?" Her arms were now crossed, her guard was up, and the battle had begun.

"You, waiting and waiting to write me into one of your novels so that you can tell the world how horrible I am!"

"Do you hear yourself, Trevor? Do you?" She pleaded for me to see reason.

"Just own up to it! You've been taunting me and playing with my head ever since. I'm sick of it, just stop!" It felt like all of my worries and fears had been piling up into a tin bucket and that they had all just come cascading out. I knew that my voice had been too loud and my final exclamation too shrill.

"Trevor, not everything is about you! I'm not playing any game with you, it's all in your head! It's with yourself!" She made a motion with her hand, as though it could physically shield her from my words, my truth.

"Oh, yeah right! Just admit that you want some revenge on me for what I did. For what happened that night." There it was. In all of the time that we were together and all of the time that we had been apart, that infinitesimal moment of time when my fist connected with her jaw was what defined us. It defined me. It was defining that moment in the store room. It was the center of the dilapidated universe that we had once built with bright planets, celestial orbs, and stars that was now off kilter and filled with the dark void of a singularity.

"What do you want me to say? Huh? You hitting me was the worst thing that could ever happen to me, it damaged me so profoundly that I'll always have you on my mind, and an axe to grind with you? No! I'm not just my past relationships, Trevor. I'm a person with a life and passions that extend beyond my own self. Are you really that short-sighted to not see that?"

Maybe she was right. Maybe I had been inventing this evil version of her in my head for so long to justify what I had done, to assuage my own guilt. Maybe I needed the game to play so that I could blame her instead of myself. I didn't have a response. My silence seemed to embolden her and bring on a new lashing of words. She didn't need to publish a character based on me and make subtle jabs or observances to cut me. She had a direct line to say exactly what she needed to without having to fuddle with subtext and plot.

"OK, Trevor." I had struck a nerve here. "I wanted to hurt you the way that you hurt me. But I realized that would give you the power. That would glamorize what you did." I could tell that she was building up to a larger comment, one that would likely rip me apart. "You're so tormented about how I might tell people about what you did? Why don't you just try apologizing, huh?" She paused as if she thought I might just blurt it out, then and there. "Say it out loud, own up to it. You say you're so sick of being haunted by this, but it's not me that you're mad at. It's yourself."

In that moment I knew that I could react in one of three ways: 1. Forgiveness, the most peace-giving of all outcomes, but might have led to some tears as I struggled with the torrent of emotions welling up in me and start to erase the villainous version of Avila that I had built in my mind. 2. Abject denial and more accusation throwing followed by a brief storming out which would leave me in a dark storeroom playing the role of the crazy ex. What if as she left in a huff, she slipped and hit her head on the slick cement of the store-room? Surely, no one would believe my innocence if she were to crack her skull and go into a coma, or die. Or 3. That I could lose control before I decided between the first two options and attack her. I didn't find any option appealing.

But Avila made the decision for me. She shook her head slowly, pitying me with her eyes and pursed lips. She left silently, just like she did many nights before. I stood in that empty room for some time, not wanting to rush after her. I debated staying in that room until closing, when I could be sure that everyone had left and that no one would see the shame, written so delicately and precisely across my face. In the few moments that passed, I decided to just make a run for it, I would try to slip out through that same narrow opening between the two bookcases.

I headed out into the hallway and could hear Avila's voice coming from the main area. I tried to find my way through the back of the crowd, but the main area was now even more cramped with all of the fans from the front of the store now loitering, shifting their weight as they stood to hear her speak. She was into a story about how her friend, the woman who had been speaking earlier, had told her about the increasing incidences of young girls being kidnapped and sold into the sex trade. Avila remarked that she thought it would make a good mystery, was it a supernatural monster snatching up these girls? Indeed, in was an ancient evil: greed.

I slowly and quietly moved through the crowd, finally catching the words at the bottom of the posters that I had been avoiding with the logo for the non-profit associated with the cause. I had been so afraid to confront her eyes, her likeness, that I neglected the most obvious of clues to the plot of her novel. It appeared to be for the relief of human trafficking in third world countries. Avila was starting to thank her friend, the woman who had been speaking earlier, for her dedicated work with the charity.

I felt like the most absolute jerk. My anxieties could have been cut off before they even sprouted if I hadn't been so proud and insistent on my victimhood.

I made my way to the exit and abruptly heard the sound of Avila's voice cut off as the door closed behind me.

As I made the short walk home, I contemplated the events of that week, that past decade. Could it be that simple? Could every song, and book, and show have misled me? Surely, if any ex would be vindictive and punitive, Avila should have been. Could it have been as easy to explain as an inflated memory, a trumped-up feeling that I was living within and experiencing every nuance of, instead of facing reality? Could a woman really just move on and wish a man well after a romantic dissolution? Where was the nervous laughter and the panicked breath? No music abruptly ended or picked up as I had approached. Could it be that she gave me no thought? Not enough to dedicate a year of writing to exact a bitter and protracted revenge.

Perhaps it was all just another game that I can't win, I thought.

Heartbreak, a meaningful career, a dead-end ambition. I can't win. I think it was at that moment that I was released.

What will I do with myself now that I am robbed of my all-encompassing distraction? The wind extinguished from my sails as I was freed from the parasitic relationship I'd constructed with my vision of Avila. Could we both be free, rid of each other, and able to move on? How true-to-life, and how anticlimactic that seemed to me. But oh, what a relief to be just someone in her past and no longer in her path.

So why am I continuing? Why are you still reading? What more could there be to say? Come on, surely it must be plain-as-day to you. You must have an itch in the back of your mind insisting that something is still off, not quite right, "doesn't add up."

You're right.

I spent that Saturday and Sunday in a deep sleep, recuperating from my week of anxiety-induced insomnia. I felt refreshed and clean. I had faced my demon and she was nothing but an apparition held in between two opposing gusts of wind, suspended between their forces, but now, swept away.

As the morning sun sparkled off of the glittering skyline, I had an unyielding sense of unease. It was a bad omen to start the work week.

Perhaps my immune system had been thrown off by the emotional roller coaster of the previous week, I thought. However, this worry was not a phantom, reverberating and demanding to be remembered. The long email in my inbox revealed that I was indeed being taunted and that my worries were founded. I had spent all of my energy on Avila that I made no room in my mind to realize the obvious. The suspect that I had been chasing was baiting me all along.

It was a note from the Traveler. With his text he applauded my efforts through veiled metaphors and back-handed asides. He had desired a worthy adversary to catch him. When he went to make another fraudulent transaction the previous week and discovered that his usual sites had been shut down, he left town immediately. He hinted at his arduous journey abroad and dared me to break all jurisdictional precedent and track him down.

I showed the message to Director Knight. He laughed at the hubris of this man and suggested that I go on and call up my counterpart at Interpol to begin tracking him. "Hobbertson, you're a competitive fellow. You run all those miles each week, and for what? Now you have someone to run after. Go get 'em."

What followed was a whirlwind of international exchanges and at least two last-minute trips to apprehend this man, only to find that he had just fled. With the ever changing nature of money laundering and the now receding boundaries of the world, I find that I am spending more time at work and traveling than at home. It is time to dismantle the life I've built in this city of mine and make the leap. I'm moving to Washington, D.C, and

I'll rent a crummy tiny apartment that I will never see. I'll finally be able to move up in my career and take the actions I need to, so that I can catch this taunting hacker.

I've spent the past few months unburying from the enormous wall I'd erected around myself. I have now read each of the Scarlett Moore novels and can say that they are indeed good. I've even watched the latest movie in the series. I don't see a trace of myself in them, but they have allowed me to re-learn who Avila was and appreciate our time together. I've learned to stop holding the opinions of other so highly and to forgive myself. I've learned to stop holding my breath for the next layer in a prolonged drama. It has ended.

When I look back now, I can see that week had been the fever-pitch. It had been one prolonged fitful sleepless night when the infection was at its worst; when the fever induced by Avila's memory was about to break. I recall that I had been in a cold sweat that entire week, my heart was beating irregularly, and my joints were tense. But now, it is over. It is a memory.

Releasing myself from the worry of Avila chasing me allowed me to realize that the man I was after, Traveler, was trying to ploy me into a cat-and-mouse game. He didn't just want to take off with the money, he wanted to have someone chase him. He needed the thrill of escape. Once I was released from the grip that I imagined, I was able to focus all of my energies on catching this man. Now he would have to worry about my motives and my next move. He would have to escape Trevor Hobbertson.

ABOUT THE AUTHOR

M.K. Williams is the author of multiple books. You can follow her for more in-depth information on these books at 1mkwilliams.com. To receive updates on upcoming book, please take a moment to subscribe.

If you enjoyed this collection, please consider leaving a review for The Games You Cannot Win. Each review helps other readers discover this book. Thank you for your support.

www.ingramcontent.com/pod-product-compliance
Lightning Source LLC
Chambersburg PA
CBHW021651110726
47902CB00007B/1914